UP SUMAC LANE

and

OTHER SHORT STORIES

Volume III

Send inquiries to:

Digital Legend Press and Publishing

Honeoye Falls, NY 14472

See the complete Digital Legend library, visit www.digitalegend.com

For info write to: info@digitalegend.com
or call toll free: 877-222-1960

ISBN: 978-1-937735-09-8

Printed in the United States of America
First Printing: November 2011 (V1)

Book interior format and cover design by Alisha Bishop

Up Sumac Lane

and

Other Short Stories

Volume III

Christmas Carol Kauffman
Compiled by Marcia Kauffman Clark

DIGITAL
LEGEND

New York

CONTENTS

PREFACE

These last few weeks I have been typing almost non-stop to be able to bring all of you Volume three before Christmas. It has been very time consuming, but extremely rewarding. We live in a wonderful day and age, when we can scan pages of books that were preserved many years ago.

If Mother were at my side helping me these past few weeks, she would most likely share the thoughts she had eighty years ago: "Who me? I had no idea that someone like me had the talent to write! Short stories for the YCC and you ask me to give you one story a month? Well, I sure hope I can come up with something the young people would want to read. My ultimate desire is that the Lord will guide me to think up stories that will touch the hearts of future readers and create in them a desire to be more faithful, more obedient and more loving and kind."

I would most likely say to Mother, eighty years later, "How in the world did you come up with all the stories that are so different? Mother, it amazes me, no two are alike!" And she would respond," Well, I don't really know for sure, but I always prayed for direction and would sit and ponder about each one. Yes, a few were from actual experiences I noticed in others lives, but most of them I just made up. I don't like to be doted over. I don't want to--- in any way feel proud or arrogant, because the Lord has blessed me with a so called "Gift." That idea makes me feel uneasy. I guess I would feel better saying it is a blessing that Heavenly Father has given me. You know, I am continually thinking up ideas for another story. They somehow just come to me. I thought I'd just be a pastor's wife here in Hannibal and support Daddy, and some how the Lord has blessed me with the strength and ability to do both. You know, I've always felt very deeply that when we do all on our part, Heavenly Father makes up the difference. We can't just sit idly by and expect the Lord to do it all for us. It takes a lot of determination and action on my part, to do it. So I just keep writing. That's my sole purpose if you boil it all down. To know that some day when I stand before God, I hope and pray that He will tell me, "Well done, thou good and faithful servant."

"I've tried to be faithful and yearned to be good; yes I often felt unworthy for some reason. I guess that's my human side. Oh well, I think all the experiences I had as a little girl and also as a young new bride, loosing my precious Norman, and then having our little Donnie, so ill, so many times, has given me the experiences that brought soul wrenching emotions, which in the long run has become a blessing to me, as I write. Oh well, I think if I had my life to live over today in 2011, I'd be doin the same thing I did back in 1930; being faithful to do the best I could do and be."

One thing about Mother is that she always had time to lift the weary of heart, to bring laughter and happiness to those who surrounded her as she served others at our little Mission church along side Daddy. She seemed to be everyone's best friend and people came to know her true self without meeting her in person because of her devotion to share her gift to others, not only within the Youth's Christian Companions but through her full length novels.

It was very difficult to see her suffer greatly before she slipped away forty two years ago this coming January. I was a young mother with an active two year old little boy, and just two months away from giving birth to my first daughter. I had no idea I would be writing a preface for a third volume of her short stories this very day.

Mother wrote the first story in this volume when I was three years old. Little did I know then the influence she would have upon hundreds of thousands of people. Today, near the end of 2011, it has been my privilege again of painstakingly attempting to read the inside edges of photo copied pages from the tightly bound volumes, so perfectly preserved in the Mennonite Historical Library. It is with much gratitude, that I share these captivating stores.

My greatest pleasure is having the wonderful privilege of choosing those most precious young people who became a member of our family when a little girl at Hannibal. Mel Lapp, thank you, loving friend of years gone by and still across the miles today, for sharing your memories with all of us for Volume III.

Many thanks to Joe Springer and Victoria Waters, at the Goshen College Historical Library, for their united effort and interest in making photo copies of each precious page. My gratitude is never ending to my publisher Boyd J. Tuttle and to his daughter Alisha for their belief in my desire to share Mothers unending influence, now forty two years after her passing. Christmas Carol, the honor is mine to continue your gift to each of us, but most of all, I am grateful for the privilege of calling you Mother.

FOREWORD

In 1953 Christmas Carol's husband Nelson Kauffman was a teacher at a two-week Winter Bible School, at our Maple Grove Mennonite Church in Atglen. Pa. I was greatly impressed by this energetic teacher/song-leader. This was my very first introduction to Christmas Carol's family. I read, as everyone else did with great anticipation, Carol's serial stories that captured my interest, along with thousands of other readers that were published in the Youth's Christian Companion.

Some months later, Brother Kauffman asked me if I would consider a period of Voluntary Service at the Hannibal, Mission Church. My friend John Smucker was about to terminate his time of service there as I was to take his place. I really struggled with this for two very important reasons to me. As a young 22 year old, I was enjoying a good life on the farm, but mostly, I had a girlfriend that was dear to me that I would miss very greatly. But, finally after prayerful consideration, I accepted the call, in October of 1952.

When I moved into the mission parsonage with the Kauffman family, their two youngest children, James age 11 and Marcia age 9 became a part of my new family along with Nelson and Carol. Voluntary service workers, Janice Bender and Esther Stoltzfus- who wrote the Forward to Volume I, also lived in their home. The two older children MaDonna and Stanlee were away at school.

Immediately I integrated into the household with assigned duties at the parsonage and within the small mission congregation there. During my 24 month stay, I drove the mission bus, picking up many convert/members with no cars, visited the state prison once a month to testify and encourage men who had became friends with Johnny Allison, and did maintenance in the home as needed.

Though Nelson gave me general instruction about my assignment there, I was on my own, while James and Marcia were my constant companions and helpers. The household was happy and fun loving with Carol's distinctive inimitable style of supervising the household; sometimes serious and off times hilarious, but always kind.

Carol was like a second mother to me, giving me counsel and encouragement to this sheltered farm boy from the east. I married my long time girlfriend, Pearl Stoltsfus, on June 8, 1955, seven days after my assignment was over and Nelson came to Pennsylvania to perform the ceremony.

We continually had company come. Some were long time friends and some were strangers, who always with Christmas Carol's generous spirit became friends overnight as they were never turned down a place to stay. Some how, Carol could find the time within her busy schedule that always included the continual writing short "stories" for the YCC. It amazed me how one tiny little woman could get so much done which also included her full length novel "Not Regina" which was first published as a continuing story in the YCC.

I wrote every day to my sweetheart back home. We kept every letter to and from each other and I often wrote of Christmas Carol's fun loving, yet profound caring personality. I immediately found myself attached to this family as we had family scripture and prayer every morning after breakfast, around the kitchen table. Often after supper we would play games. I remember playing Blind Men's Bluff with the table pushed next to the stove and also as we stayed gathered around the table, we would make up stories as we passed the papers folded down from the top after we each wrote our own sentence. We continually had laughter with Carol around! One of the most enjoyable games that Carol created from her ingenious mind is now available with a modern day name "Word Possible" available through Digital Legend Press. This is one you will for sure want to have for your family, for all ages, whether young or old.

Throughout the rest of their lives, Nelson and Carol Stayed in touch as dear friends and mentors. Their untied devotion to God and the Church was a great inspiration to me. The friendships began with the children in Hannibal with the Kauffman family. Marcia, you've come a long way from that nine year old girl who sat on my knee at family worship and family celebrations in the Kauffman home. I am proud of you for keeping your mother's legacy alive with this third Volume of Christmas Carols short stories. God has blessed me with countless precious memories of a godly lady who followed the Lord and whose influence is unending.

Mel Lapp
Kinzers, Pa.

Up Sumac Lane

By Christmas Carol Kauffman age 43, Hannibal, Missouri
Originally published July 22, through November 18, 1945

In this issue we begin a new continued story by Christmas Carol Kauffman. Those who remember Lucy Winchester will hail with pleasure this new serial, Up Sumac Lane, *beautifully written and interestingly developed from actual life. That "Truth is stranger than fiction," is once again confirmed. The story will continue indefinitely, but likely will not always appear week by week because of the four page issues which are published biweekly. Save your copies from week to week, and enjoy the possession of the entire story when it is completed.*

—Editor.

There was more than one reason why Philip Spalding cleared his throat very, very slowly and swallowed hard. It was very unlikely that the boys on either side of him heard the deep breath he drew, but Philip looked over at the small freckle faced lad on his right and to the red headed boy on his left, but both, like all the other children in the assembly, had their eyes fixed on Miss Wilmot on the platform.

The story ended. One hundred and twenty nine children, who had been sitting spell-bound for fifteen minutes, gave vent to their actions by making some kind of stifled exclamation when the climax came. The runaway lad had come back home, and his mother had walked out to the gate to meet him. Miss Wilmot found her place with her class of big girls at the back of the room. Hers was the best story of the week. Maybe it was because she put expression into every word. Whether or not it had been a true story, she made her characters live, up to the end, when the mother folded her son into her arms, some of the teachers quickly wiped away little wet spots that had splashed onto their dress fronts. Miss Wilmot's story was a touching one.

Philip Spalding was watching the young lady at the front seat who was sitting in the midst of the small children. She too had been weeping. One tiny black-eyed girl, scarcely five years old was standing on the bench, and her little arm, not too clean, was by her teachers arm,mussing up her pretty dress. Two little boys in blue jeans were tramping around with mud on their shoes. On her lap she was holding a blond headed little youngster who had fallen asleep on Miss Wilmot's lap earlier. His head was making a wet spot on her sleeve. About a dozen more little folks were squeezed into the same bench, all of them desiring the envied place the little black-eyed girl had today. They took turns sitting next to their teacher.

"Why would any boy ever want to run away from home and mother?" Mused Philip, still looking at the teacher of the smallest class on the front seat. The superintendent had taken his place on the platform to make some announcements, when one little girl on the very end of the bench fell off backwards and bumped her head. Instantly Angelena Fairfield put the sleeping one on the bench beside her to rescue the one who was hurt. She had her hands full. Her assistant for some good reason was absent today, and Angelena had sixteen wiggling, twisting, preschool children to whom she must try to teach the story of Moses. There were other teachers in the school who undoubtedly were more experienced in teaching than she was, but Angelena Fairfield had been the only one who had volunteered to teach the baby class. Philip Spalding did not know this.

How can she stand it? he thought to himself, *those youngsters messing over her like that?* They crumpled her dress and pulled on her belt, they fumbled with her collar, and one little girl pulled out her hairpin, tried it out in her own hair, and then stuck it back, jabbing Angelena in the scalp, (not purposely of course) and she only smiled and replaced it at a more comfortable angle.

I wonder, went on Philip with his thoughts, *if Mother was patient and gentle like unto Angelena Fairfield is with those youngsters? There weren't sixteen of us, but there were ten! I wish I could remember Mother. How could a boy run off and grieve his mother? Angelena---I suppose she has a mother---and a father too---at least I hope so. I hope she hasn't felt that loneliness I've always known, for there's something about her that's different and sweet. I like the way she does things. I like the way she walks and the way she---*

The passing bell rang, and the boys in Philip Spalding's bench got to their feet. So did he.

"Don't push, Jack," he reached toward three boys, and tapped Jack Applegate on the shoulder.

"I wasn't pushin', that was Dick."

"Well, stand back boys, and wait your turn."

The baby class passed first. In her arms Angelena Fairfield carried the towheaded child who woke up from his nap and was still in a daze. His wet head lay in her warm neck. By the hand she led one, and two clung to her skirt. Her twisted belt became undone, and her brown hair hung around her ears in little ringlets. It was June, and warm. Philip Spalding's heart pounded as he watched her he pass.

"Boys," he began as soon as they reached their classroom, "That was a good story Miss Wilmot told upstairs a while ago wasn't it?" I guess boys such as me who never had a mother; think if they only had one they'd really be good to her, but---

"Didn't you ever have a mother?" Asked Percy White, the meekest boy in the class of nine.

"Yes, but I can't remember her," answered Philip with feeling. "I was just a little boy when she died. I hope you'll all go home today and do something nice for your mothers. She cooks meals, and makes your beds, and mends your clothes and does---

"Mine don't," broke in Rodney Painter, "Mom don't never make my bed, or mend my duds." Philip looked at Rodney's split shirt sleeves and dirty knees showing through his busted pants. "Mom's never home 'nough to thread no needle," he added with an explanatory tone.

"Now, open your notebooks," said Philip with strange compassion in his voice. One week of teaching a class of boys in Bible school in a city church was a new experience for Philip Spalding. Could it be possible that there were other boys besides Rodney Painter, who had mothers---flesh-and-blood-mothers---who didn't care enough for their children to make their beds and mend their clothes? Did Angelena Fairfield have children in her class, little baby children, who were neglected like Rodney was? Maybe one of those little ones was Rodney's brother or sister. Maybe Angelena knew. Maybe that was why she was so patient and gentle to them. Maybe that is why they clung to her dress and she didn't care. Philip had never known anything but love even though his mother died when he was less than three and his father had gone to meet her when he was twelve. His big sister had tenderly cared for him and his tiny baby brother. Jenella was like a real mother to them all. She mended their socks and sewed on buttons. She wrapped up bleeding fingers and soaked stubbed toes. Jenella had sat on the floor and played blocks with him sometimes, and had tied rag stripes for his kite tails. Jenella could bake fluffy white bread and make as good corn cakes as any boy would wish for, but Jenella wasn't his mother.

There was more than one reason why Philip Spalding cleared his throat very, very softly, and swallowed hard that warm morning in June. There was an unspeakable longing, an immeasurable craving in his heart to have a mother with whom he could discuss questions, but since he knew this would never be, his yearning went toward that young woman on the front seat. Strange he had never felt this way before. In fact, Philip Spalding had never before seen a girl who made him feel like Angelena Fairfield did. He couldn't actually explain it, nor did he try. It was there unsolicited. He didn't shake it off. He didn't exactly want to either. There was something about Angelena that made him want to be a **better** man than he had ever been. She seemed to be the kind of a girl with whom he'd like to discuss things---anything. He had never talked with her, and wasn't sure how her voice sounded until it came her turn to take the platform during the story hour.

"This morning," announced the superintendent smiling at the children, "Angelena Fairfield will tell a story. Let us be as quiet as possible," Phillip held his breath, with admiration as he watched her to the end. Once she looked at him, but only for an instant. Philip wasn't sure that she saw him. He liked her voice and the bright sparkle in her eyes as she spoke. He liked the waves in her light suntan hair, and the way he felt. Calm. He liked the way she smiled down at him, and more than that, the story she shared was confident and real. She was a real Christian, without shame or pretense.

More than ever, Philip Spalding felt calm, feeling his dead mother's prayers. He had been reminded by Jenella, that both their mothers had been godly, praying women, something he hoped for at church, for which he had vowed his allegiance to. He desired to be the best he could be. Angelena took her place on the front bench, and little ones surrounded her on both sides, crawled up into her lap and the others as close as they could get.

"Say, Angelena," Philip Spalding had finally met her face to face at the side door of the church. He spoke with mingled feelings, "I think you got the worst class in Bible school."

Angelena's hand went to her throat and she answered with surprise, "Do you think?"

***

Chapter 2

His face got hot and he loosened his shirt button. Why had he said it that way? That isn't what he had intended to say to Angelena. No wonder she looked surprised. He had waited a week to have a chance to speak to her, and now he had said the wrong words! He was ashamed and disappointed in himself as he walked to his car and started for home. His mind was in turmoil, and the farther he went the more embarrassed he felt. Before he would have a chance to share what he actually meant to say, Angelena was the last person on earth that he intentionally would want to treat blunderingly, and would inform an unfortunate opinion of him. Philip threw his books on the seat beside him. He tried to whistle, but that didn't help. He stopped at the filling station for gas. He wondered where Angelena was staying so he could explain himself. Maybe he would accidently meet her, wherever she was staying. Maybe he could meet her at the side door and hopefully, finally make it right. But this was Friday and he would have all afternoon, all day Saturday and all day Sunday to live under false pretence.

Philip Spalding harrowed corn all afternoon, but with every step of that long walk up and down the rows, he kept repeating what he had really meant to say.

"How was Bible School this week? Philip was asked.

"Not too bad and not too good," he answered without looking up.

"You're not as enthusiastic about your class this year. Do you enjoy it?" asked his sister Louisa, handling him a dinner roll.

"It's okay," answered Philip dryly, trying desperately to hide his disappointed emotion.

"It's quite an experience trying to teach a class of city boys. Several of them acted out badly today. Sometimes they test my patience and I don't know exactly how to handle them." Philip tried to laugh, "Rodney Painter is a pill, but I guess it's not his fault because of what he comes from. He spends most of his time running the back alleys near his home.

"Say, by the way, could I invite three or four of the Bible School boys to come along home with me sometime? The woods are full of wild flowers now, and we could go fishing, or have a wiener roast up on the hill over the falls." He turned and looked at Jenella, the oldest sibling in his family.

"Whatever you want to do, Philip," she replied. "It will be alright with me; just let me know the day they will come so that I can have supper made. The strawberries will be ready to pick this coming Monday and if the warm weather comes we may be picking by Wednesday. How about having them all come this next Wednesday?"

The weekend seemed like a full week to Philip. Monday morning came, and once more he was in his class with the mischievous boys on either side. Angelena took her place with her brood of children clustered around her, and in the group were two new pupils. They looked anxious and timid, and on the verge of tears, among so many strange faces. Angelena was doing her best however, to assure them they would have a nice time in their classroom downstairs. There would also be yummy cookies!

Philip lingered at the side door where he had met Angelena Friday noon but she did not come by. As soon as school was dismissed she had escorted her new pupils to their homes several blocks east of the church. Philip lingered till everyone was gone, and concluded that the girl he longed so much to see, might have gone to the parsonage before he reached the side door. Was she trying to avoid him? Had he offended her that badly? Nervously biting his lips, he walked swiftly to his car without looking back. Just as he drove off, Angelena Fairfield went singing around the corner of the church.

Tuesday came and went, with the same disappointing experience. Bible school closed, and still Philip Spalding had failed to speak to Angelena. It would have been seen as forward or daring as some other boys seemed to be around the girls, and he probably could have forced himself into her presence, but Philip was not the bold type. No one could have called him cowardly, or weak-kneed, but Philip Spalding was timid and reserved, especially so, when he thought of someone as fine as Angelena. He was not the kind to go into raptures over people, or talk fluently with strangers, but his manner was a quiet one. Nevertheless, Philip Spalding was constant and steadfast in his devotion to God and firm in his convictions. Those who learned to know him admired him. Sometimes the glib of tongue was likewise more fickle. After watching Angelena Fairfield day after day in Bible school, Philip was convinced she was a woman as special as a rare jewel, and, although she was not conscious of it, she had made a wonderful impression on him for good. The influence of her being followed him day and night. In fancy, he talked with her over and over, and corrected his blunder. At night he met her in his dreams. More than once a day Philip talked to God about Angelena. "Dear Lord, if she is not the woman I think she is, please help me to forget her now and forever."

"So, you didn't get to bring your Bible-school friends along home one time?"

"No, Jenella, "answered Philip, hanging his hat on a hook in the hall. "If I'm fortunate enough to teach next year, I'm going to put my bid in early. They had plans made for every evening. I talked to Karl Normandy first, and he said he couldn't come, so I knew it wasn't any use to talk to any others."

Philip plowed corn. He cleaned the barn, curried horses, milked, put up the hay, worked on the binder, and got ready for harvest. Even at these tasks, he never forgot Angelena. Sometimes he was so lost in reverie that he did not notice when someone spoke to him. An irregular train of thoughts about Bible School, and the little children clinging to a sweet faced young woman, filled his mind most of the time.

One night in July, Philip Spalding sat in his room with his open Bible on the table before him. He had just finished reading a chapter in Romans, but so deep had he been musing that he scarcely knew a thing he had read. He opened the drawer of his desk, picked up his pen, and began to write. He sealed, addressed, and stamped the letter, put it in his Bible, turned out the light, and threw himself across the bed. The moon, a huge, luminous disk, shone down on his wind-blown face, and he could not help but wonder if Angelena, in the city, could see that same great shiny satellite. Maybe not. The houses there were close together. With the same kind of a spirit that gives a poet or composer inspiration to write. Philip fell into a peaceful sleep.

Angelena held the letter in her hand and a puzzled look crossed her face. She went directly to her room, opened the letter and read:

Dear Angelena,

You will be surprised to hear from me, but I want to apologize for something I said to you five or six weeks ago in Bible School. I told you I thought you had the worst class in Bible school, but I did not mean it the way it sounded. What I wanted to say was that, I thought you had the hardest class. As I watched you, I saw you had your hands full. Really, I think you had the BEST class in Bible School instead of the worst, for no one else could have managed it as you did. I sincerely wish to ask your pardon.

Very truly yours,
Philip Spalding

Slowly, Angelena folded the letter and returned it to the envelope. For some time she stood at the east window, looking down the avenue toward town. A stream of cars, glistening in the midday sun, moved on and on---never ending.

"Well," she whispered softly, tucking the letter in the dresser drawer, "I'll answer, but not for several days."

***

Chapter 3

Philip waited. Day after day, he watched for an answer to his letter that he hoped would bring some consolation to his troubled mind. He was beginning to think that he had make a mistake, and was going to the table with a lost appetite, when at last it came! His older brother brought it in from the mailbox and handing it to him, said with an inquisitive smile,

"Looks like a lady's handwriting, Phil."

He took the letter and hurrying to the far corner of the porch where he could be alone and opened it with his pocket knife, and intently, with excitement read:

Dear Philip,

*I was surprised to get a letter from you. I do appreciate your attitude, and I rejoice because you are conscientious. You need have no regrets about your remark, for I believe I understood you completely. I took it in the way that you meant it. I thought more about it because I **knew** you meant that I had a hard class to handle. I guess it was a lot different than yours. But thanks for your kind thoughtful words. I am sure we both enjoy teaching, and with any trying situation, we can come to the Lord in prayer. I praise God for that.*

I wanted to tell you that I enjoyed the story that you told all the children. God bless you.

Sincerely,
Angelena Fairfield

Sure! The letter pleased Philip, and he buttoned it up in his shirt pocket so he could read it again. He walked with haste to where his family was waiting. The bread tasted better than it had in days, yes, much better than it had in weeks.

While retiring for the night, Philip read the yearned-for letter again, with painstaking care lest he should miss a word. *She did not say she was glad to hear from me or that I should write again,* said Philip to himself. *She did say she appreciated my attitude and thoughtfulness, and she asked God to bless me, and that really blesses me a lot. I want God to bless her too. I wonder what all she does at the parsonage and how long she will be there?*

A few weeks later Philip felt moved to write another letter to thank her for the part of her letter that thanked him for his thoughtful words.

May God bless you and reward you for what you are doing in the city. I wish you could see my two pet squirrels. I feed them with a medicine dropper. I am sure you are busy in the city. I am busy cutting and gathering in our wonderful crops. Sometimes in the evening when I am not too tired, I try to write poetry.

I'm always remembering you in my prayers, and know you are doing a wonderful work among the children of the city. How long will you be there? I would be very pleased to hear from you.

Very sincerely,
Philip

Would she answer again? Would she? She did reply again and Philip was very happy. She was wrapped up in the work of the Lord. She told of visiting the sick and aged, and she was involved with visiting in the jail services and typing sermon outlines for the pastor, baking pies for company, teaching Sunday school pupils, preparing for upcoming revival meeting, and praying for all who came to listen.

One evening during the revival, Philip walked into the church just in time to hear Angelena sing a special song. She saw him enter and take a seat about four rows from the back.

Two young men came in with him. Those were likely his brothers. After the meeting was dismissed, Angelena shook hands with people throughout the church, and Philip Spalding was one of them. The next night he wrote another letter.

Dear Angelena,

Last night's meeting was wonderful. I enjoyed the sermon and the song that you helped sing. And I hope to come again one night next week.

I am sending you an Indian arrow I found while shucking corn yesterday; it is the smallest one I have ever found. I am a great lover of nature, and many a time I've stood on a 300 foot bluff not far from my home with my back against a tree, thinking. There is something about being near nature that draws a person closer to God. I thank God every day that I was born in the country.

***

The next letter Philip received from Angelena, she invited him and his brothers and sisters to a social that was to be held at the parsonage:

We have arranged a Christmas program and we want to draw names and exchange gifts---not expensive gifts. Nothing should cost over a quarter. Do you think you can come?"

Philip answered, "We will be there if at all possible. But, I would like to say that the best Christmas gift I could wish for would be a picture of yourself. I know I do not deserve one, but if you have an extra one you would care to give me, I would be very happy.

Angelena did not have an extra picture, so after considerable deliberation she made a pencil sketch of herself and sent that. "I was also born on a farm," she wrote, "and I am a great nature lover, but God has called me to walk the sidewalks of the city. Before long, I hope my parents can come to visit me, for I dearly love them and you would too if you knew them."

Philip and some of his brothers and sisters attended the social at the parsonage, and the following week he wrote---

Dear Angelena,

I'm glad we got to come to the social. I enjoyed it, but all evening I longed to have a chance to exchange a few words alone with you. There was such a crowd, and people in every corner of the house. I prize the lovely pencil sketch you make of yourself, but whenever you can, please send me a snap. If I ever get the privilege to meet your parents, I know I shall like them, for they have one grand daughter.

***

Philip saw it in a window in a small town not far from home. He stood there until his coat and hat was white with snow, then he went inside.

"This will make a lovely gift," said the clerk taking the bill out of Philip's hand.

"If you can," said Philip with a delighted expression on his face, "I'd like you to wrap it ready for mailing."

"Of course, I will."

With a song in his heart and a song on his lips, Philip hurried to the post office and sent the package. With new vigor, he hurried home to finish the work of the day.

"Here's your sack of flour, Jenella," said Philip opening the kitchen door with the sack on his shoulder.

He wasn't expecting a letter today. It must contain something special. With trembling fingers he opened it.

Dear Philip,

You will be surprised to get another letter from me so soon, but I have an awful burden on my heart. For days now I've been weighed down (Philip caught his breath) with this question. Is it the leading of the Lord that we should continue corresponding? I am convinced it is unfair for you to keep writing when I feel as I do. This is my honest conviction. (Philip felt sick and dizzy.) I don't want to run ahead of God in anything. If the Lord so leads and makes His will plain, I shall be glad to correspond with you again, but for now it seems unwise to me. I have appreciated your friendship, but remember, I wrote to you only as a brother and friend. I hope you understand. It is late already. The Christmas rush is on, and I must retire so I have strength for tomorrow's duties. God bless you and keep you happy in Him.

Sincerely,
Angelena

Philip got cold and then hot.

"Jenella," he called back over his shoulder, "I'm going upstairs for a while. I don't believe I want any dinner today."

"Are you sick?"

"Well, sorta."

She heard him close the stair door and, hurrying after him called up, "Can I give you something Philip?"

"No. Never mind, Jenella, I'll be all right after a while, maybe."

Philip stumbled almost blindly into his room and closed the door softly. Sinking into the chair beside the table he unfolded the letter and read again those heart-breaking words. He buried his head in his hands with his elbows on his knees. Philip Spalding had experienced a few disappointments in the twenty-one years of his life, but never had he experienced defeated hopes like this. Had he been deluded in his young woman? He had not questioned her sincerity. He had been confident that God was leading them in their short friendship, and now---now in her sixth letter she doubts the leading of the Lord? She is weighed down and burdened with uncertainty? OH! The package! The first Christmas gift he had ever purchased for a girl and now she--- Oh NO! It thrilled him so to buy it---to write her name on it.

"A special package for you Angelena", the minister's wife called from the open door.

Angelena came bounding.

"Oh, it must be a box of candy from home! I know that is what it is." Eagerly she cut the string and unwrapped it without looking at the postmark.

"Oh!" Angelena caught her breath. "Oh!" she repeated and her lips trembled. Her cheeks got crimson.

***

Chapter 4

"What's the matter, Angelena?" Asked the minister's wife, perplexed over the girl's reaction. Her tone and face showed distress---or disappointment; which was it?

"Oh, Sister Brinton," answered Angelena, in a very troubled voice, "How can I accept it?" It's not fair. I---I can't accept it."

"But why, Angelena?" Asked Mrs. Brinton, stepping closer. "It's beautiful!"

"Of course it's beautiful" agreed Angelena, and I've always wanted a little cedar chest like this!" It's prettier than any I have ever seen, and look at the beautiful stationary in it. "But, it's from---" She stopped abruptly while tears welled up in both eyes.

"Who?" Whispered Mrs. Brinton.

"I know who," answered Angelena, "but, I simply dare not accept it. I---I just wrote and told him." There were footsteps on the porch. Hurriedly, Angelena grabbed the box, paper, and quickly ran up the stairs and fast as her legs would take her.

***

"Here's your mail, Angelena," A little child stepped into her room. It was the pastor's child.

"Thank you Geneva. Come in,"

"No, Mama said I should come right back down." Not saying anything, she left Angelena in her room. There were two letters. One in a long blue envelope from her mother, and one from New Hudson. Angelena opened the last one first. Leaning hard against the windowsill, she sighed heavily and read:

Dear Angelena,

This little gift I am sending you for Christmas, if only a small expression of my appreciation for you. Your friendship has meant more to me than I can ever tell you.

You cannot begin to imagine the impression your life has made on mine, Angelena. Everything about you is different from the ordinary. When I saw this little chest in town a while ago, I could not keep from getting it for you. I am in the post office here in New Hudson now. I need to hurry home to get to work. You will find the little key in one of the envelopes. A happy Christmas to you, and may God bless you, my cherished friend.

Very sincerely,
Philip

Tears blinded Angelena's eyes and her heart pounded violently. "It's awful!" She sobbed, "But I can't possibly accept it when I feel like this." That afternoon Angelena went about her work as if she had been stunned by a sudden blow. One minute she was tempted to recall the contents of her last letter, but the next, she felt confident she had done the right thing. There was one thing she was determined that she would not do, and that was to pretend she cared for someone when she wasn't certain. She knew she admired Philip Spalding as a Christian; she knew the man had unquestionable character; he was clean cut, handsome, and she could not lay a finger on any one thing that repulsed her. He was interested in spiritual things and was talented; she was sure of all that, and yet she could not feel an indisputably sure leading of the Lord in this new friendship. Angelena was sad all day. By evening she felt weak and unstrung. The pretty hand carved cedar chest was put away in the bottom dresser drawer.

Dear Philip, (she wrote with a deep sigh. She rubbed her forehead and continued with a quivering hand.)

I hardly know how to begin this letter, because my thoughts and feelings are all mixed up. Your letter came this noon and also the gift. The chest is beautiful, but it makes my heart ache, for I am afraid I cannot make you understand me. I'm not sure if I understand myself sometimes, and I wouldn't blame you if you thought I was the most terrible person on earth. If my last letter hurt you, please forgive me. If we could talk face to face a little, I believe I could explain myself better. Letters can often cause some awful misunderstandings. You got my last letter after you wrote the one I got from you today.

Do you really and truly have a conviction that we should keep writing? I have been sad---all afternoon for some reason. The cedar chest is way too pretty for me. I do not deserve it at all. I wish you would frankly tell me if you feel God wants us to keep on writing. If we go on and it is against the will of God, it will not make for happiness. For that reason, it must be God's will for sure.

God bless you, and I hope you have a very happy Christmas.

Sincerely,
Angelena

***

Dear Angelena,

This is Christmas day. Some cousins and aunts took dinner with us. I hardly know what to write, but feel an urge to do so. I'm not sure that I should tell you my convictions now, but I think I should just wait on the Lord. We will make no mistake by trusting Him as our guide. My only desire is to do His will---nothing more or less. I would love to talk to you face to face, and until that time comes, let me tell you just one thing, Angelena. Whether I ever hear from you again or not, since the day I received your first letter on the 29th day of July, your life has been a constant inspiration to me, and because of you, I am a better man than I was before. Regardless of the future, the few letters I have received from your hand are priceless to me. I will miss hearing from you, but this will only drive me oftener to my knees. All I have to say now is, forgive me if I've ever written anything I shouldn't have. God bless the loveliest girl I have ever met.

Very sincerely,
Philip

Angelena tried to act happy and carefree. She worked, she sang, she prayed, and each time she ended her prayer, she felt compelled to admit to her own soul that Philip Spalding, a fine man as he was, was to mean nothing special to her. She tried frantically sometimes to make herself believe this was of the Lord. Only when she was all alone and the lights were turned off, would she allow herself to question this belief. Each day she became more firm in it.

One evening in January, Angelena answered the phone.

"This is Philip Spalding speaking."

"Yes."

"I'm in town on business and if I may, I'd like to come out to the parsonage to talk to you a little,"

"All right." Angelena trembled.

She met him at the door. He swept the snow from his shoes and removed his hat.

"Take this chair, Philip." She sat across from him. It seemed hard for him to speak. The young man's heart pounded within him. How beautiful and neat as a pin Angelena looked in her yellow housedress and white apron!

"Are you here alone?" He ventured timidly.

"The baby is asleep, but Brother and Sister Brinton and their little girl have gone to a funeral. It sure has been one grand winter day."

"Yes it has," answered Philip, but it mattered little to him what kind of day it was. All that mattered to him was the girl he came to see. If she would only tell him she was sure it was God's will to write again---let it snow or blow or thaw. He came purposely to ask her, and here he was now. He must ask her, before anyone came in.

"Have you---" at least that much was out. All the way to town he had tried to decide how he should say it. His voice trembled. "Have you thought more about it, Angelena?" He tried to smile. His breath came faster and faster. "About corresponding, I mean," he added.

"Well, yes, I have," she answered, brushing her apron over her knee. "I feel we should drop it all together--- at least for the present. I can't tell you why I feel this way. It only seems to be God's will. I hope you won't feel hard toward me, but I want to return the cedar chest you gave me." So saying, she went upstairs.

Philip stared at the wall. For a moment he forgot where he was, and something like a storm cloud seemed to envelope him. He heard Angelena's footsteps on the stairway---coming down, down. It made him feel as if an elevator was taking him into a dark shaft. His heart pounded in his ears.

She handed the package to him. It was wrapped in the same paper he had mailed it in.

"I cannot keep it." She said softly, "Though it's very, very pretty."

Philips tongue was paralyzed. Somehow he got to his feet and stepped to the door.

"Goodbye." He spoke sadly, as in a dream.

"Goodbye." Angelena closed the door.

"My God---my God," groaned Philip as he opened the car door, "give me strength to drive home!"

***

Chapter 5

Misplaced confidence has wrecked many a worthy soul. Philip Spalding had implicit faith in Angelena Fairfield's sincerity. To doubt the motive for any of her actions would have seemed to him such a discreditable thought that he would have counted it a sin. Her letter had seemed so thoroughly unadulterated and true to her personality, as she had said it in their short acquaintance that he would have staked his life on her judgment in any matter. But the last letter upset him terribly. And this jolt affected every nerve in his body. He had had hopes because she had written, *Maybe if we could talk face to face, I could explain myself better.* And he had put forth special effort to meet her face to face. He could have transacted his business in New Hudson, but he had driven twelve extra miles through the snow to see Angelena. Her explanation had been short and with such a tone of finality that Philip couldn't have voiced his honest conviction had she asked for it. He was ready to say frankly what he thought God had revealed to him, but what was the use? Philip Spalding was too unobtrusive a person to insist on a hearing.

The little hand-carved cedar chest lay beside him on the front seat. The beautiful gift which he had purchased and given as a symbol of his unspoken love---his secret love, which to him was as sacred as his devotion to God---now seemed like ashes wrapped in ugly brown paper. He could not bear to look at it. He shivered. His teeth chattered, and he madly gripped the steering wheel---but he was not angry. He was not vexed. He was not indignant. Philip Spalding was bewildered. He was hurt. The wound was more painful than if he had received a bodily injury. His hopes had been shattered, and the sharp splinters were stabbing him in the heart. He drove westward. The snow was falling fast. Instinct must have led him on the right road, for part of the time he felt numb and senseless. For twenty miles he nosed is car into the storm, then suddenly he was out of it. He drove straight to the bluff, and with the brown package under his left arm and a tire tool in his right hand, he climbed to the top. Under a fur tree he dropped on his knees and clawed away the snow with both hands. With the tire tool he gouged out frozen leaves, rocks and hard earth until he had made a hole about nine by fourteen inches wide and ten inches deep. In it he placed the box and covered it with cold clods, sticks and wet leaves, and then beat snow on top of it. He did not shake with sobs, but with deep groans; he stood with his back against the tree and looked out over the valley below. He had stood at that tree before and had received inspiration to write poetry, but now, all he could do was pray with deep-throated sounds, which best expressed his grief. If he would ever write another poem, it would be a sad one about shattered hopes and faded dreams. Slowly Philip went back to his car and headed for home. There was no rankling bitterness in his heart toward the girl who had disappointed him. To wish revenge never entered his mind. Though he could not understand her recent decision, he still thought she was beautiful and good, and hoped God would spare her from anything that would bring pain or discomfort.

A month went by, and Philip still caught himself praying for Angelena. He saw her face on the walls of the barn, on the fields, and in the clouds. Then this is what he wrote one night:

Dear Angelena,

You won't be expecting a letter from me since you said it's best for us not to correspond, but I want to write just once more, to tell you that since you are such a good girl, you may be blaming yourself for hurting me. Do not do it, for I am not worth it. I'll admit it hurt, but that was only because I could not understand; I was **sure** *I was right. For several days and nights I lived under the blackest of clouds and I prayed and prayed God would reveal His will to me, and always the answer came that I was right. Then one night a song came to me, "After the shadows, there will be sunshine", and suddenly the darkness left. I am living in the light now. You said we could still be friends, so this is just a friendly letter. Nothing more. A friend is one who holds us to our best selves and that is what you have done for me. I never expect to have the privilege of doing any personal favor for you, but I will always be praying for you. Tear this letter to bits, if you feel like it, and if you don't like what I have written, forgive me.*

Only a friend,
Philip

Angelena stepped into the clothes closet, and buried her face in her blue checked apron. She burst into tears. For some reason she did not tear the letter into bits. In the back of the closet, was her little trunk. She opened it and got out a bunch of letters bound together with a green rubber band. After reading the letter once more and replacing it in the envelope, she made a small figure in the upper left hand corner.

For a little while, Angelena held the eight letters bearing the postmark, New Hudson, and then she tucked them away in her trunk. She washed her face and went downstairs to finish typing the sermon outlines Brother Brinton had given her that morning.

She finished the one on "Prayer," then another one on "A Clean Heart," and started on the next, Angelena's hands stopped, and she scanned the paper at her right. She picked it up and read the subject: "How God leads." Her heart throbbed, not as with pain, but as it does when one is suddenly confronted unprepared. She was glad that Sister Brinton was busy in her bedroom.

1. He leads by circumstances, conditions, events, states of affairs, facts, and incidents.

- *Details of life over which we have no control.*

2. He guides by His Spirit. The meek, he will guide in judgment: Psalms 25:9

- *The difference between leading and guiding*
- *To lead means to proceed, pilot, direct, steer, show the way, point the way,*
- *Go ahead, superintended. He leads boldly-Illustrations*
- *To guide means to direct thinking, as with a guide book to mentally influence, or educate to choose the correct way.*
- *He guides mentally with His counsel, Psalms 73:24*
- *He will guide you into all truth, John 16:13*
- *There is a difference between feeling, self-gratification and being led by God.*

3. He leads by His Word, "Seek first the Kingdom of God"

33

• No one can go entirely by circumstances, for they are often contrary to Gods will.
• The Spirit never guides contrary to the Word of God.
• "Commit thy works unto the Lord." Proverbs 16:3
• If any man wants to know…
• The Word never leads to disaster.
• The Word leads to honorable ways.
• With the Word and the Spirit united, it will all correspond. One can be sure.

Summary---The unraveling of every tangled knot in life and the solution to every problem is found in God's Holy Word.
• He leads by circumstances boldly- there is no mistake.
• He directs our thinking.
• The Word of God is a sure guidebook.

Angelena sat wrapped in thought. I'm here, serving in Raytown, doing the kind of work I love." Not a thing at home had prevented her coming here. She felt led to answer the call. Circumstances let to particular events that had taken place, and she found herself addressed by Philip Spalding one day last year. She had not planned it or anticipated what happened, but that first letter he wrote after seeing him more than a month---it wasn't necessary to apologize for that little thing. It was just open correspondence. Did she ever anticipate his first letter? She had not planned it or anticipated it. Who is Philip Spalding anyway? Yes, everyone spoke so well of him. But how does she know or did she know he was her ideal? He had very kind eyes, but how did she know they could cry too? Angelena Fairfield had an ideal. How could she know she could find it in Philip Spalding? She wanted to know for sure!

He seems like a genuine Christian, she thought to herself, *and he did write me nice letters and I really did love that dear little cedar chest, but if I had kept it, he would have thought I really cared about him and I---* Angelena began to type again, thinking, *I know I don't, and it's not right to pretend I'm glad.* She typed to more words. *I'm glad. I'm glad I gave it back.* Angelena bit her lip to keep back the tears. "I am!" she said to herself.

***

Chapter 6

Angelena fell sick. The doctor called it a deep-seated cold and gave her strict orders to stay in bed for three days after her temperature was normal.

"What have you been doing?" He asked, taking her pulse and watching her carefully with true professional observing.

"My usual work," answered Angelena, closing her eyes.

"Are you worrying over something?"

What a question. Why did Doctor Cox think she might be worrying? Angelena drew a deep breath, and sighed wearily, "Not that I know of," she answered, trying to make the question sound absurd.

The doctor saw her eyelids jerk and said with the air of a wise judge, "You seem rather nervous."

"Oh well," put in Angelena with a disapproving laugh. "I'm naturally of a nervous disposition, Dr. Cox."

"Yes, I'll leave a prescription." He walked to the door and picked up his hat. "Stay on fruit juices as long as you have a fever and---" he looked back over his shoulder as he opened the door, "you quit your fretting."

Angelena said something under her breath that was as disapproving as her laugh. She felt just a little crusty toward Dr. Cox for implying she might be fretting. The idea! What would she be fretting about? Angelena Fairfield was branded as a cheerful, sweet-tempered, optimistic person. She hated it that Sister Brinton heard the doctor ask her such a question. Even though Angelena was sweet-tempered *that* rubbed her fur the wrong way!

"Listen, Sister Brinton," ventured Angelena with a tinge of a petition in her voice, "please, please don't think I am worrying or fretting over anything, because really truly I am not."

Sister Brinton opened her mouth to speak, but forthwith, her words failed her, and Angelena continued with a cloak of true devotion wrapped around her words, "I am perfectly satisfied here; I love the work, and I'm not homesick, and there's not one thing that is distur---I mean, Sister Brinton, you mustn't worry about me. I'll soon be rid of this cold and be feeling fine. "I've had lots of colds already."

"Well, I'll do all I can for you, Angelena," answered the woman, stepping backwards toward the door. "I'll send some fruit juice up right away and go to the drugstore and get this prescription filled then. Are you comfortable?"

"I'm alright. I hate to be such a bother,"

"Don't call it a bother, dear; think of all the kind things you've done for me already. You just take care of yourself now."

Sister Brinton seemed a little reluctant to leave Angelena for some reason. Was it duty, sympathy, pity, love or what was it that made Sister Brinton look at Angelena the way she did?

"I'll soon be all right," repeated Angelena, trying to smile even though her heart beat fast from fever.

The Spalding homestead was a spacious two-story frame structure with long porches on three sides, and bordered in front by an expansive yard. The house stood back from the main road about four or five rods across a creek, and there was something about the location and surrounding scenery that gave the place a friendly, relaxing, homelike appearance. After the death of Father Spalding, which at the time seemed most untimely, his four brave-hearted sons who were old enough to bear responsibility, determined to pull together and keep the home their parents had worked so very hard to get, and preserve that family life they had established.

Philip was twelve, but there are numerous tasks about a farm that a twelve-year-old boy could do, and Philip Spalding stood ready to do his share with his four older brothers. Jenella, still in her late teens when Mother died, had proved her ability to supervise the work in the house for nine years prior to her father's death. He had taught her how to rotate crops, how to raise chickens, ducks, pigs, and cattle; how to calculate, invest, budget, and face reverses. Perhaps he had a premonition that he could not stay with his family; at least he left something with his ten children that bound them together with an inseparable cord of love, and the boys from big Hubert down to little Romie looked to Jenella for everything from shoe strings to advice about new parts for the tractor. The sisters, four of them, worked in and about the home in harmony and peace, and it was little wonder the neighbors said, "Beats all, how them Spalding's stick together 'thout no pa an' ma."

Philip loved his home, the house where he was born, and lived and worked twenty-one years. He loved every one of his brothers and sisters, and every square foot on that farm he'd helped to save. There were favorite spots in the barn where he and his brothers had played hide-and-seek. They had played blacksmith often, and shoed the old sawhorse out under the mulberry tree. They had dug for worms behind the hen house, and under the grape arbor, and gone fishn' all day with Agnes and Mollie, an' et Jenella's 'lasses cookies, fried chicken, an' buns, an' rolled 'roun on the sand while they all listened to birds an' things.

Philip knew the names and habits of every bird and animal and creeping thing that lived on or near the Spalding farm. He loved life without any artificiality. He loved the country, but his thoughts went more and more toward a certain house in Raytown. In the bustle of it all, a bright-faced girl stood out before him like a lone star.

Philip had often gone to Jenella for help with a knotty arithmetic problem, but to ask her advice now was something hard to do. It wasn't that he didn't trust her, but his problem was such a personal one. He waited for weeks before he found himself in the right mood, and Jenella alone in the living room.

"Is there anything to dreams, Jenella?" He asked, leaning against the library table and fumbling with some keys in his pocket.

"What kind of dream do you mean?" Jenella looked up from the sock she was darning.

"Well, it's like this:' Philip swallowed hard and looked out over the snow-covered lawn. He crossed his feet and cleared his throat, "One night I dreamed I saw Angelena Fairfield's mother and father and." Philip coughed and shifted his position, "I was at their home and shook hands with them, and it was so real, I can't forget it."

"But how did you know it was them? You've never seen her folks have you?" Jenella dropped her darning and rocked back in her chair. Philip ran both hands through his hair, "No, I've never seen them, but somehow I know it was them, and they smiled at me in such a way that I---oh, well listen, Jenella…" Philip walked to the window and looked out.

He turned abruptly and said with a queer little laugh that wasn't natural, "Guess I'm silly, but maybe I can get it off my mind now since I told it." So saying he started to whistle and left the room.

"Philip," called Jenella softly.

"Yes," he stood in the doorway.

"I wouldn't put much stock in dreams."

***

Chill rains came with March. One afternoon Jenella asked Philip to go to New Hudson for some sewing machine needles, and he was glad for a chance to use the car. Before leaving he went to the woodshed and filled an empty vanilla bottle with coal oil. He drove straight to the Bluff. The road was muddy, so he parked the car in an off-place and got out. He used the same tire tool he had used two months before. The melting snow was seeping down through the sticks and stones. The paper around the chest was crisp with frost. With his bare hands, he tore it off and lifted the lid. On top of the stationery lay the little brass key. He did not touch it. His heart pounded and his entire body shook with emotion. A little rabbit hopped past the fir tree and startled Philip. In a trembling hand he held the bottle up and with one great cry, poured the contents on the open box.

"Never," he said, "never shall a living soul see it!"

He struck a match, and stepped back.

***

Chapter 7

Philip watched the angry flames do their destructive work. He folded his arms tight across his breast to hold back the throbs of strange pain that shot through his heart. The pulsations were not due to any heated feelings or excitement. It was not with any spirit of animosity or disgust that he decided to burn the little chest, but the happiness he had felt on that memorable day when he mailed it to Angelena was an experience so sacred to him, but at the same time it did bring pain to watch the chest kindle and char and vanish away. Some boys would have saved it for another girl or given it to a sister, but Philip couldn't have done either. No one knew of his purchase and it was best to do away with it before the rains soaked through the snow. Angelena had never answered his last letter, so again it was best to destroy it. Philip didn't want it in the house.

Disappointments either harden or soften a man. Some people become bitter and critical, while others become more tender and gentle. Some balk or refuse to try to live a Christian life, while others seem to have their finest traits polished to brightness a that never was seen before. After the last flame had died out, Philip covered up the hole in the ground and looked out over the great valley three-hundred feet below him.

"Oh, God of the hills," he prayed, lifting his eyes, "take my life and make something out of it. Keep me from sin---great or small---and lead me in the way you want me to go. I don't ask to have my own way; only show me what **your** will is for me."

"Prayer is the soul's sincere desire, unuttered or expressed," and in Philip Spalding's sincerity, he called on God in true humbleness of heart and with adoration. He had not prayed any other way since the day he first learned how, from Jenella, but as he grew older he grew in understanding as well as in stature. In the past several months Phillip had prayed as never before. No one---not even Jenella---guessed his soul's struggles.

***

Angelena's illness was neither long or serious, except in her thinking. She and herself carried on more than one conversation. The first day she was out of bed she sat by the window with a sheet of paper on her lap. The magazine under the paper was full of meaningless marks from her pen.

"Dear Philip", she wrote. She looked out over the streets below, gazing steadily at nothing in particular. Brief sighs escaped her parted lips, and suddenly she went back and forth across the two words with her pen and tore the paper in two. A much needed letter in Philip's mind never came his way.

Spring came. Everything living was permeated with exuberance and with new vitality; and Philip Spalding was not immune to it. When Brother Brinton wrote and asked if he would consider teaching a class of boys in Bible school again in June, he replied buy saying, "If you think I can fill such a place in your school, I am willing to try. There is plenty to do on the farm during that time, but my brothers said they can spare me for something like that."

Philip sat on that same bench and watched Angelena with her class of kindergarten children up in front. The months that separated them had marred neither her beauty nor her charm. To Philip she was more appealing than ever. There was something about her personality that to him seemed irresistible. Once she met him in the aisle of the church and she smiled and spoke. The air smelled sweeter to Philip that day, and God seemed a little nearer. All the way home, something hung over him like a benediction at the close of a church service.

For several nights Philip tossed on his bed and prayed for sleep. Weary and sad, he got up and lit candle. For some time he sat at a table in the corner of the room, his face buried

41

in his open Bible. He had read the twenty-seventh chapter of Proverbs three times before going to bed that night and had marked verse five with his pencil. The clock downstairs struck one.

He wrote with a longing heart—

Dear Angelena,

If ever a young fellow needed help from God, I do tonight, for I am torn to pieces. If I could only somehow have a chance to talk with you once, then maybe I could help you understand how I feel. I wish I could look into your heart and read what's there. Sometimes I think I can, and yet I can't.

Angelena, I must make a confession. In Proverbs it says, "Open rebuke is better than secret love." I beg Father in Heaven, and you, to forgive me if I am doing wrong, but I love you. It is not a secret now, for I have told you, but not in the manner I have longed to. I think you must have known it all along. It hurts me to tell you, but it hurts me worse not to tell you. I am not a rich man. In fact, I do not have a single thing but love to offer you. I have prayed and prayed that God would guide me right and lead me to my life work. I feel weak, but whenever I see you, I get new inspiration to be true to God.

When I was only four years old, God called me to serve Him and I cannot get away from it. You may never return that love that I feel for you, but whether you do or not, I cannot sleep tonight until I have told you that every day in Bible school when I see your pure Christian face, it draws me closer to God. I know I have no right to be writing you this after you returned the cedar chest and said we shouldn't correspond any more. Maybe I'll never give this letter to you, but I am going to pray earnestly that if it is God's will, I will give this to you tomorrow, if I have the opportunity. If not, I will know it is not God's will and I will burn it.

Someone told me your parents are well-to-do, but I am only a poor farmer boy without a mother or father, and I'm not brave enough to tell you this face to face, so I am writing it. I heard yesterday that you are going home for a while after Bible School is over, and before you go far away, I must tell you that I love you. I am not ashamed of it. If there is an answering call in your heart at all, let me know, and if not, just keep me as a true friend.

With pure love,
Philip S.

Philip folded the letter, sealed it in an envelope, and closed his Bible on it. Exhausted in body and mind, he threw himself across the bed.

When a person's mind is troubled with a serious problem, sleep often chances or relieves its confusion. Sleep did neither of these for Philip. The love letter under the Bible expressed what was in his heart when the shades of night were drawn, and again when the morning light appeared. He was sure of his love for Angelena night and day, and he was sure he wanted to express it.

The moment he was awake he began to pray that if it were God's will for Angelena to get the letter he had written, he would provide an opportunity for him to hand it to her. If it was not God's will, he asked that the way be closed. Philip Spalding had faith in God, and he had faith in his own prayers. He prayed as he milked the cows; he prayed as he drove along in his car. Just at the edge of Raytown the right front tire went down. Philip was disappointed, for he wanted to get to the church early today. That would be his most likely chance of meeting Angelena, for she was usually one of the first ones there. Sweat dropped from Philip's face as he worked on the tire. It was almost time for the opening song when he started down the avenue. His hands were dirty and there was a black spot on his shirt sleeve. He was trying hard to be reconciled to the answer to his prayer, for he was sure now he would not get to speak to Angelena.

He jumped out of his car and ran to the parsonage to wash his hands. He stopped short and listened. He heard singing from the open windows of the church.

"Oh, pardon!" Philip caught his breath. He almost bumped into someone just inside the door.

"You're late too?" Laughed Angelena. "I forgot my enrollment cards and had to come back."

"I had a flat tire and---and I've got to go and wash my hands."

Angelena was on the porch already.

"Angelena," he called softly. She turned. He stepped close to her and with a trembling hand held out the letter.

***

Chapter 8

It was afternoon before Angelena had a chance to be alone. One could read a letter from home in the presence of half a dozen girls perched on beds and chairs and window sills---girls discussing anything from corn to what they thought of Philip Spalding and Karl Normandy---but hardly a letter the like of which Angelena Fairfield had tucked in her dress pocket. When Philip had met her so unexpectedly at the door several hours before, and handed her an unstamped, sealed envelope, she had no other place to put it. She had hurried to the house without a purse or book in her hand. Occasionally during the morning session, the letter crackled

44

slightly, giving her assurance she hadn't lost it. And what was it that Elva Glassenapp was saying about Philip Spalding being so nice, but bashful? Angelena caught her breath and nervously pinned back a stray curl, while her eyes expressed respectful dread and curiosity. It was not her disposition to be meddlesome or inquisitive about another's affairs, but what was Bertha Milladay saying now about Philip? She thought he was handsome and refined? The letter crackled in Angelena's dress, but little did anyone of the girls suppose this truth, or that she agreed or disagreed with what was being said. While her heart pounded like a toy drum, she kept herself busy doing this and that.

The call for dinner brought the conversation to a sudden hush, and Angelena managed to be the last one out of the room. Quickly she pulled the letter out of her dress pocket and snapped it in her purse. It was after two before Angelena went to town. That day at the dinner table Brother Brinton had announced that the next evening the workers would all eat supper in the park or in Mr. Vincent's rock garden, and among other entertaining features of the evening, Angelena Fairfield would give a reading. Selecting a chair at the very end, she sat down and opened her purse. Breathlessly she opened the letter.

***

More than once Philip Spalding was breathless too that morning. Both wonder and fear gripped his heart after he had given Angelena the letter. Not by any outward manifestation could he have guessed what her reaction was, and he had watched for it as much as he dared. He went home that day wondering, hoping, doubting, believing, dreaming, and praying. Yes, Philip Spalding believed in his own prayers, and hadn't God answered graciously, and given him an opportunity to meet Angelena alone? Wasn't that divinely

45

planned that she should forget her cards and he should be detained exactly as long as he was? Philip tingled with sheer joy---yet wonder and fear took sudden hold on him.

Prolonged sighs escaped Angelena's lips as she read those words meant only for her. Once a faint smile lit up her face, and once she brushed away a tear. "I've prayed that God would guide me right and lead me," here Angelena caught her breath and held it. Once before she had read similar words. Yes, Brother Brinton's sermon outlines. Could it be that Philip knew how God leads and guides? Could it be that he was right? "I've prayed and prayed," she read again and turned to the next page. Half numb, she sat wrapped in deep thought. Was it true that God was leading Philip boldly, and guiding his thinking?

"I really wish I knew," she said to herself, "but I'm afraid if I answer he'll give back the cedar chest, and I really don't know if I love him. "He *is* nice," she mused, "He may be quite wonderful, but how do I know? I'm afraid I might be disappointed. But--- he must care for me," and she started all over and read the letter again. After she got home she put a small number 9 in the corner of the envelope, and put it in her trunk with the others.

In four days Bible school would be over. Four days passed by and Philip received no answer. Eagerly he watched for it. He came to Raytown each morning with new hopes but each time drove home disappointed.

Philip had been disappointed before. He knew what it was to have his expectations unfulfilled. He knew unsatisfied longing. But even though he felt familiar with that emotion, it became even stronger.

The first week in July, Philip received a postcard from the Postmaster at Plumville, informing him that a letter bearing his name was there at the post office and was being held for postage. At last it came, eight days after it had been written.

Dear Philip,

I dare not tell you how long it has been that I wanted to answer the nicest letter ever sent to me. I believe the Lord is blessing you, because you asked Him to be with you every day. It has been three weeks since I left Raytown. I am home now and it still seems a little unreal. Today my father showed me all around the farm. Our wheat this year is the best crop my parents have planted in years. Whoever informed you that my parents are well to do is mistaken. They are far from wealthy, but we do have a comfortable home and all. We have never known anything but hard work and hard times.

Philip, I must be sure. I must know Gods will for me and I will gladly follow that. I also want you to know for sure the call from God that you feel you have, shows true sincerity. I know He will guide you and provide all your needs. I think I understand you and I want you to know you have been a blessing to me also.

Sincerely,
Angelena

***

Dear Angelena,

Perhaps you did not know you failed to stamp your letter, but it finally arrived today after I paid for the stamp, Do not feel bad about it Angelena. I am sure for some reason you forgot to put it on.

May the Lord give you a real vacation because you deserve it. You can't imagine how it made me feel when you wrote and told me how your parents showed you around on the farm. I am not making my plea for sympathy, but I miss my father and mother more than ever before. I was too young to remember my mother, but I miss her too. Be good to your parents, Angelena. I know you are; but so many young people don't realize how much a father and a mother mean to us until they are gone. These are busy days for us. Since Bible school we have put up 12 acres of wheat, plowed 27 acres of corn and half of another 14 acre plot of clover.

It means so much to know that you pray for me and you can be sure that your name is often whispered in my prayers for you also. I trust God as never before and know He will guide me. I want to be true to Him. Philippians 3:10 rings in my ears. "That I may know Him." I desire to be conformable to Him and His will for me. I know you understand my desire along with Heavenly Father.

Sincerely,
Philip

He did not tell her in this letter that he loved her, but yet there was love in every word. She did not write any answer to the love he offered her. She did say that she would be glad for a chance to talk with him. She did not say she would be glad to hear from him---but she did write that it was the nicest letter ever written to her! Could it be that she is receiving a letter from another? Why hadn't he dwelt before with that thought? She did say---"I want you to know you have been a blessing to me also." That did make Philip happy. It made him happier than any other letter she had written before. And she did say that she thinks she understands me!

Before it was dark Philip drove over to the Bluff. He stood with his back against the cedar tree and his feet resting on the spot by the few ashes that were left where the pine box was buried months before. "I am so blessed to know Him," Philip whispered as he looked out over the valley and watched the quiet dusk settle in the fields below like a soft blanket---"and the fellowship of His suffering," he repeated softly.

In the distance he heard the sweet sound of a whip-poor-will.

***

Chapter 9

Philip accepted an invitation to accompany some friends to a church conference to be held near Angelena Fairfield's home. He accepted enthusiastically, and told Angelena in a letter that he might be coming. He was about to leave when her short letter came that informed him saying---"You can spend the night in our home." Philip was thrilled.

This new kind of adventure to be in her home and meet her parents is usually thought of as a bold undertaking like a tiger hunt or a trip to a foreign country. Although this trip could not be compared to anything like either, it was a remarkably exciting occurrence in the life of Philip Spalding.

When Angelena met him at the close of the last session of that big convention and introduced him to her parents, he was overcome with a tender feeling of solemn wonder that he could hardly speak. When he did speak, his voice was not as he usually sounded. There was an unmistakable likeness to the characters he remembered is his dream. He has quite forgotten it until he was trembling with surprise and reverential fear that comes into the presence of a divine partnership when they shook hands. He hardly knew for a moment whether he was dreaming or awake. Angelena did not understand the reason for his manner and little did she realize why his hands were trembling.

"You may go with my father Philip," said Angelena looking up at him, "and I must find our car. We'll meet you at the gate."

They all met at the gate a few minutes later. Then came two young women full of talk and laughter. They talked and laughed all the way home. When they reached her home carloads of guests followed them into the house. Her father ushered them into the living room which was full of chairs, and soon every single chair was taken. Angelena served delicious lemonade. By the time Philip was sipping his, he was trying to figure out how he could have a chance to talk to Angelena because there were so many people around. Everyone else has plenty to say, so Philip sat listening to everyone, but his ears heard only Angelena speak. When there was finally a pause in the prolonged discussion in the Fairfield home, then he heard Brother Fairfield's suggestion as to where everyone was to sleep.

Philip was given a cozy little room to himself. Although he was tired, he couldn't relax. The bed was comfortable and the pillow case smelled like honeysuckles, but he was not sleepy. He lay wondering over the short time with Angelena's parents and the persons in the dream that he had many months ago. It was a dream he wanted to share with Angelena. Would she be interested in him or would she think he was some strange creature? Perhaps she already thought he was strange because of the way he acted when they first met them. He really wanted to tell her about it so she would know how surprised and happy he was so that she wouldn't just think that he was plain stupid.

In the morning he went walking in the yard. The smell of bacon and biscuits came from the open kitchen door. "Good morning," Philip jumped. He saw her on the other side of the rosebush.

"Good morning," he answered smiling. "Picking a bouquet of roses?"

She smiled, "Aren't they beautiful?"

"Yes they are." He answered, stepping a little more towards her.

"Hello out there," a voice called from the kitchen.

"Yes Mother,"

"Daddy wants those cuff buttons, and they're in the room where those girls---"

"Alright Mother," she said almost scampering to the house, and Philip was left alone by the rosebush with the rest of his sentence still in his month.

Breakfast was served and then they had family worship. Angelena and her mother were busy as two bees, doing up the morning's work and making preparations for another day at the conference. Angelena's two talkative friends gave joyful assistance, and Philip could hear them laughing in the kitchen while he talked with Mr. Fairfield on the porch.

Soon they were all on their way back to the conference where there was a multitude of people. Philip was happy to have been in Angelena's lovely home. He had not been disappointed in her parents, but he was strangely lonesome, lonesome in the midst of people, lonesome for a certain girl who was behind him in the back seat of the car.

"Thank you for your hospitality," Philip was saying after they got out of the car, when he felt a sudden slap on the shoulder, and he turned and met the face of Karl Normandy.

"Spent the night at the Fairfield home?" He asked with a broad smile.

"Well, well, let's sit together and chat a while before it's time to begin. We'll have about five minutes if my watch is right. How are you doing anyway?"

"All right, Karl. How are you doing?"

"Very well; very well. If present plans carry, I'll be a married man by fall."

Philip swallowed hard.

"By fall, you say? And who is the fair lady? Let me ask."

"Her name is Phyllis Carver from Michigan. I doubt if you know her."

"No, I don't."

"You got a girl?"

Philip got hot, and for a moment his heart burned within him. He felt a poke in his side, and Karl whispered in his ear.

"Does it mean anything that you were at the Fairfield place tonight?"

"Time will tell," answered Philip, blushing. He bit his tongue. He was hardly home from the conference when a letter came.

Dear Philip,

I love the Lord, and I want to be true to Him. The past cannot be changed, but in the future I want to be careful to take God's way to happiness, for there is no true happiness except by God. I cannot exactly express my feelings, but I am pushed by conviction to tell you what God has made clear to me. It makes me sad, but I cannot wait any longer to tell you honestly, after praying for wisdom, that I have come to the conclusion, I cannot be more to you than a friend.

In my mind it is wrong for a girl to let a friendship go on, and let the other one be thinking hopefully, when she does not have the same hope. Love must be divine. I would be a very sinful creature it I tried to go on with you, not knowing it was from God. I know you are a praying man and I believe you are willing to accept the will of God. That gives me courage to tell you my honest convictions.

I admire you as a Christian, and your sincerity has inspired me and helped me. I do not want to bring sorrow or grief to your heart; and you too may feel this way now. I pray that God will someday bring a dear sweet girl into your life who will truly love you, and be a deserving helpful companion to you. I have no plans for the future except that I am going back to Raytown soon, and expect to throw my life into the Lord's work there.

When you were here I thought I would tell you a few things, but something said "Wait." There were two things in the past which for some reason seemed to be evidence to me of God's leading us together and because of that, I know I am to still be your friend and I want to be your friend. Please do not be bitter towards me. I wish you all that is good and may God bless you.

Sincerely,
Angelena

Philip waited a week to answer.

Dear Angelena,

God has made it possible that we can come to Him, the Great Master of life, and pour out our hearts with full measure we will be heard. He does not always answer as we wish, but He is always near as we seek him. I have been brought very near to Him lately. You did not say I should not answer your most recent letter. To my knowledge, I have received three letters from you in the past that I did not answer.

Recently I read this in a book, "The roses that fall about our path are not blown there buy misguided winds, and the rocks that fall upon our path are not thrown there by some careless explosion that was accidently set off. Every one is wafted to us from Heavenly Father's hand, to give us cheer and every blow is directed by that same hand as we are battered upon the anvil of His predestined purposes into the instrument of His own use."

This has helped me. I do not understand the "why" of a lot of things, but time will make all things clear.

Angelena, I knew all the time that I wasn't worthy of you. I thought honestly that I was being led of God, and I am glad you felt free to write your honest feelings. Divine love is the only kind I want. We must be true to God if it takes the last breath I have, but I am not sure of myself, because I am weak. Though I dare not tell you enough times, I still think you are a very dear sweet girl, and you have definitely helped me to be a better man. My dear devoted father and mother have given me a name that is far more than all the riches of this world, even though I am only a poor boy.

What must your parents think of me? I can't finish thanking them for their kindness. They are lovely people--- both of them. I was hoping I would, and I did feel comfortable when I was in your home. Somehow I was in a daze and could hardly believe I was there. I longed to tell you something then, Oh, well, it's past and over now. I still have a little slip of paper in my billfold that I carry around, that answers my prayers.

HIS ANSWERED PRAYER

He asked for strength that he might achieve;
he was made weak that he might obey.

He asked for health that he might do greater things;
he was given infirmity that he might do better things.
He asked for riches that he might be happy:
he was given poverty that he might be made wise.
He asked for power that he might have the praise of men;
he was given weakness that he might feel the need for God.
He asked for things that he might enjoy life:
he was given life that he might enjoy all things.
He received nothing that he asked for, but received all that he
hoped for,
Because his prayer is answered and he is most blessed.

I thank God tonight for answered prayer in the past and yet to
be.
May God bless you, my friend.

Sincerely,
Philip

***

Chapter 10

Many of the real things of life are not seen; they are felt. Love, hate, dread, pain, joy are not things one can see, but they are felt and they are real. One can imagine experiences, but it is different when they actually happen.

The Bible is not merely an object made of cloth, paper, glue, and thread, so long, so wide, so thick: it is more. Truly the Bible is a book to be seen and handled, but the most important part is its unseen quality. It is a mysterious channel through which the thoughts and will and truths of God become a part of us. That makes us real.

Faith is confidence in that which is invisible, the evidence of things not seen. We feel faith without seeing, and it is one of these very real things in life. Without faith, Columbus would never have discovered America. Without faith, Livingstone never would have opened a new continent to civilization. Without faith, the religious reformers would not have accomplished what they did. Faith is a mighty force, and those who grasp it, lay hold on something which is able to make them mightier than they themselves can. Faith takes God at His word and trust with deep feeling, without seeing.

For days and weeks, Philip Spalding searched his Bible for something on which to lay hold that would increase his faith in God. Since the day of his conversion he had loved God with all his heart, and had never once doubted the call he had received from Him. Even now he did not doubt that. The assurance that he was born for a divine purpose has been a real thing in his life for over twenty years, and yet he wanted reassurance, a new and fresh assurance. He had been so confident of his love for Angelena and so sure it was of the Lord, and now she too felt she was sure it was not of God. And Angelena was a praying Christian. No wonder Philip felt weak. Self-confidence may be used in either good or bad sense. Philip Spalding had not gone to college, but he was far, far from stupid and he knew full well his confidence must come from God. Of himself he was confounded. He worked hard on the farm as if it were all his own. He attended faithfully all the services at the little country church where he belonged. He carried a small Testament in the hip pocket of his overalls and read whenever he found time. He read it through. Then one evening while leafing through the Psalms, his eyes lingered on two verses. He read them over again, "Shew me thy ways, O Lord; teach me; for thou art the God of my salvation; on thee do I wait all the day."

Philip had read those words before, and no doubt the minister had often quoted the entire chapter before his congregation, but now they took on new depth of meaning for him. He knew it. He felt it, and it gave him enough self-confidence that he could face the world unafraid and unashamed. Yes, he believed he could even face Angelena Fairfield. His conscience was clear before God, and He understood him if she didn't. He worked as never before both on the farm and in the church. He did whatever he was asked to do, and with a willing heart. And Philip prayed! But, he did not pray for God to give him Angelena. In fact he prayed for God to make him be willing to forget her entirely. His greatest desire was to live in such a way that someday God could use him. His childhood call from God was one of those real things of life that although he could not see it, he felt it very definitely.

Philip went fishing with Dale, his seven year old nephew. "Uncle Philip," began Dale, throwing his line out with a whiz, "were pals, aren't we?"

"You bet we are," answered Philip with a twinkle in his eye "but why do you ask that?"

"Well," said Dale, watching his line and smiling until his entire face beamed, 'we work and play together, don't we?"

"Yes."

"And we like each other pretty good, don't we?"

"Yes," Philip smiled.

"Least ways, you're my favorite uncle." And just then Dale took his eyes off the line for a moment and gave Philip a look of admiration.

"Your favorite uncle?" Asked Philip in surprise. How's that? Don't you like Uncle Herbert and Ronnie?"

"Oh, yes I sure do, but I've always liked you best 'cause you take me along places and carry me on your back through weedy places, and across rocks an' stuff, like that picture of the Good Shepherd we have at home, you know."

"Yes, I know the picture, Dale," answered Philip, "but I could *never be your Good Shepherd.* Jesus is our Good Shepherd, --- yours and mine too!

"Yes, I know, but you lead me by the hand and teach me how to do things. Oh, look! I've got a bite!"

"Sure enough. Here---let me. Look at that Dale. It must weight three pounds!"

"And when I get big," said the little fellow as he watched Uncle Philip unhook the fish with nimble fingers, "I want to be just like you an'---an' do things like you do---everything."

"Why, Dale," spoke Philip, catching his breath with his open mouth. Then he chuckled in such a serious thoughtful way that Dale thought he must have said something Uncle Philip didn't like.

"You don't want me to be like you? Huh?" Dale was squatted down on one knee, looking up into Philips face with an innocent boy fashion, "Just grow up and be any old thing?"

Philip was strangely touched. Something within his soul rose up to meet this challenge. This unexpected question called for an answer.

"Dale," he said at length, as he looked into those two big brown eyes, "I must be very careful how I live if you think that much of me. Then under his breath he added, "I never knew how much I could bless him, and please help me Lord to be every inch an example of the Lord."

One frosty morning, Philip got a letter from Raytown. Before he opened it he knew that it wasn't Angelena's hand writing, but it made him curious in spite of himself. According to her last letter, she had gone back months ago to the work she loved the most.

Dear Philip, he read--- it was from Brother Brinton.
The next time you come to Raytown, stop by because there is something I would like to talk over with you.

What could Brother Brinton want me to talk to him about? Curiosity became an excuse to go to Raytown before many days passed.

"Good morning Philip." Brother Brinton gave him a hearty handshake. "Come into my office and take a chair. I am glad you came, Philip." Brother Brinton pulled back his chair and sat down by the window. He looked at Philip earnestly for a few steady moments.

"I have a job for you," he said, "for a man like you."

"A job?" Philip asked, looking up in surprise.

"Do you suppose your family could spare me using you for a few months during the winter?"

"I don't know, Brother Brinton."

"Well, it's like this, Philip. For some time I have had a conviction that I should speak to you about this. We need a young man to help out in the work of the Lord here, and if you are interested in finding some experience along this line, it may prove valuable to you in the future."

Philips body tingled. The future? What did Brother Brinton know about his future? His mouth was open but he did not speak.

"I have noticed in you," went on Brother Brinton very thoughtfully, "some very fine qualities."

Philip caught his breath, and held it. What qualities had Brother Brinton noticed? "Otherwise you may be sure I wouldn't have asked you to come here for this talk. I believe there are young men like you who've never had a chance to go away to school, as much as they would have liked to, and who like you, are just as much interested in the work of the Lord and the church."

Color came into Philip's cheeks, and he crossed his one leg over the other.

"Have you ever felt that you should consecrate yourself---or perhaps I should say, give your life over to the service of the Lord?"

Philip Spalding's very soul burned within, for it seemed that Brother Brinton's eyes were looking right through him. What should he answer? What could he answer, but the truth?

"I tell you, Brother Brinton," began Philip, meanwhile rubbing his one hand down over his arm. His voice quivered a little. "I rather hesitate to say this, but when I was only four years old, I know God called me to do something in the future. I," he looked down rather timidly, "I didn't know what I was to do, but it never left me, and I do know that I can't forget that experience."

"The Lord bless you, Philip. You are the type of a man I am looking for, to come and live here in the parsonage and"

Philip caught his breath, but Brother Brinton continued---"to teach a class of boys and go along with me to the hospitals, and jails, and learn to do personal counseling. You'd find it to be the greatest joy in your life."

He smiled.

"Have you ever experienced leading a soul to Christ?"

"No sir, I haven't."

"Also, I need someone to lead prayer meetings when I must be away."

Philips heart pounded. He had never done it.

"And that isn't all! There are many opportunities to witness for Christ in a place like this. If you would be interested in finding a job here in this little town, providing they could spare you on the weekends, we could give you your board and room for the care of the church, and firing the furnace in the home. It would not be a money-making proposal, but you might be able to earn something and gain some experience. Does it appeal to you at all?"

Philip drew a very deep breath. "I would very much but---"

Brother Brinton waited for him to finish. It seemed he was struggling for words and could not find any.

"Do you feel you are needed at home?" Inquired Brother Brinton.

"Well, not so much that," answered Philip softly, "they could get along without me during the winter months, especially if I would help them get a large amount of wood stacked away, but---but," I, I'm afraid there is one person who wouldn't want me around." Philip ran his hand through his hair and looked away. He had to look away.

"Do you mean Angelena Fairfield?" Asked Brother Brinton.

Philip nodded slowly. He looked down on the floor.

"Well, I got in on a little of that. I understand there is nothing between you now?"

"Nothing," he answered.

"You mean it would be difficult for you two to live in the same house?" Brother Brinton asked a direct question, and wanted a frank answer.

"As far as I am concerned," answered Philip, holding his head up. "I believe I can face Angelena any time and anywhere. I'll admit, I thought about and cared a lot about that girl at one time, and I still think a lot of her, but I know I am nothing to her and I will keep respect for her and keep my place. It nearly got me devastated, but God has helped me live above it. I know God loves me and has forgiven me, if I have missed the mark. I know He has. I am committed, Brother Brinton." Philip Spalding stood tall, "To leave my life in God's hands. I know He's going to lead me in the truth, and teach me the way. It might be harder than I think, to live in the house with someone for whom I have cared very deeply, but I would try not to let it bother me."

"Then you mean you will consider coming?"

"Does Angelena know about this?"

"I doubt it very much. I might have mentioned it to her, but I am not sure."

"That's the part that bothers me. She may be very much opposed to having me around."

"I have never ever heard her express any such dislike for you, Philip."

"But, but I could not come, unless I knew she didn't care."

"Shall I find out?"

"No indeed, not while I am here."

"Of course not, of course not," answered Brother Brinton quickly; but, I will find out in some way and let you know."

Philip felt a little relieved. "I must know for sure," he said, "that Angelena does not object in any way." It wouldn't be fair to her. I could not come if she objected, even a little bit."

"I understand, Philip, I wouldn't want you to come either, if she objected, even a little bit. It wouldn't be fair to either one of you."

"Perhaps she has a friend," ventured Philip.

"I couldn't say," answered Brother Brinton. "She doesn't---at least not that I know of. You go home and talk it over with your family, and think it over, and I'll let you know what I find out."

Philip lingered at the door.

"I must know for sure." He repeated.

"Your decision depends on that?"

"Mostly, yes."

***

Chapter 11

Brother and Sister Brinton together, decided to ask Angelena.

"Oh!" she exclaimed, clasping her hands and looking at both of them sincerely, "It will be perfectly all right with me if you want to ask Philip Spalding to come here,"

"It wouldn't bother you then?" Ventured Sister Brinton, "Not in the least?"

"Not in the least! I'm sure it wouldn't. I have absolutely no personal interest in him, and he knows it; and I'm—I'm quite certain he feels the same toward me. At least it is no use for him to care because it will never do him any good."

"Do you think, Angelena," asked Brother Brinton, "that Philip Spalding is a real Christian?"

Angelena answered with firmness in her voice, "I know he is; and he has talent too. Experience in work like this might mean a lot to him. I want you both to know what Philip Spalding is---I mean I am not one bit interested in him and never will be. As far as I am concerned, he can come here, and I will keep my place and go right ahead with my work as I do now, regardless of what may have been mentioned before."

"Very well then, Angelena." This was what Brother Brinton said as he walked toward the door. He had no reason to doubt her. She had been a girl of exceptionally fine character and had always been frank and honest since the day she came into their home. Her sweet disposition had won her many friends among both the young and the old. Her beautiful soprano voice had thrilled many a heart. Angelena could speak in public, and she could speak personally to souls in trouble. She could cook and bake and sew and operate a typewriter. In fact what Angelena Fairfield could not do wasn't worth mentioning. The entire congregation had been blessed by her presence and work among them. So valuable a worker had she proved to be, that Brother Brinton felt he could not afford to make her unhappy or uncomfortable by inviting Philip Spalding into the home. And so he wrote Philip a letter to inform him that it mattered not the least to Angelena should he decide to come.

"I'm going," said Philip to himself. "Such an opportunity may never come my way again. "And," he added with definiteness in his unspoken words, "I'm going to treat Angelena as though I never did care for her. I'll show her I'm there on business for the Lord only. Oh, I do want to be a man, and I do want God to lead me and teach me what I should know." And with such thoughts in his mind Philip packed his suitcase to go to Raytown.

***

Leon loved him from the start. Leon, that very backward five-year-old son of Brother Brinton's, was on Philip Spalding's knee before night came and what little boy wouldn't crawl upon a man's knee if the man couldn't tell stories of foxes, and dogs, and rabbits as Philip could? Real stories, too, that happened right on his own farm where he played house with Mollie and Ronnie out under the rose arbor an' ate ripe strawberries straight from the patch without being washed, and drank make-believe tea, and went fishin' by the pond, where Mollie fell in and got all wet. Why wouldn't Leon think Philip was the most wonderful man who ever came to their house, when he could yodel, and make whistles out of sticks, and funny crawling toys out of Mother's empty spools, and tie all kinds of knots, and imitate all kinds of birds and animals, and do things that even his own daddy couldn't?

When little Leon would look up at Philip with wonder and amazement in his eyes it made Philip recall what his own nephew had said months before. Angelena caught herself listening sometimes.

"Mama!" called Leon one evening from the dining room where he was lying on his stomach with both elbows fixed so he could prop his face in his hands, "Don't you think Philip can do the mostest different things of anybody in the world?" Mama Brinton laughed, and answered something that satisfied her little son, and reminded him it was time for him to go to bed.

"Do it once more, Philip," begged Leon.

"Mama, listen to how the *hyots* go."

Angelena's hands on the typewriter stopped for a moment.

"Now you must go to bed, Leon."

"No."

"Good night," Philip reached down and stroked Leon's head.

"Mama!"

"Yes?"

"Can I go upstairs and sleep with Philip?"

"Oh no Leon, you're not used to sleeping with anyone. You might kick and keep Philip from resting."

"No, I wouldn't, Mama. I would just lie there and think about what all I'm goina do when I get big, till I fall asleep. You don't care if I come up and sleep with you, do you Philip? I bet you want me to, don't you? See Mama? He shook his head yes."

"You may do it just once then, Leon, but if you disturb him you must not ask to do it anymore."

Leon did quite well in being quiet, for his mother had told him repeatedly he must go to bed and not talk.

"Say," whispered Leon softly.

Philip looked over to the little fellow in bed.

"I'm getting bigger and bigger every day ain't I?"

"Yes."

"How many times must I go to bed before I'm as big as you?"

"Oh, lots of times, Leon."

"Six times?"

"More than that."

"Nine times?"

"Way more than that. Hundreds and hundreds of times."

"I don't want to wait that long. I want to be as big as you tomorrow."

Philip laughed.

"Well, just close your eyes now and every morning you will be a little bit bigger than the day before."

"That much?" Leon measured about five inches with his hands.

"Hardly," "Listen, your mother said you shouldn't talk if you came up here."

"I wasn't. I just whispered."

"Yes, but she meant whispering too."

"But I'm not bothering you, am I?"

"Not very much. Just a little. Now close your eyes or she won't let you come up tomorrow night."

"Close them like this?"

"Yes, only keep them shut."

"How long?"

"Until morning."

"I wish I could go along with you and work at the stove factory,"

"You can when you get big."

"Big like you?"

"Yes."

"O.K."

Leon was soon fast asleep.

Philip wrote his letter home and studied his Sunday school lesson. Before he crawled into bed he knelt and prayed. In his prayer he could not help but ask God to bless the life of the little boy with whom he was going to share his bed, for at that age, he knew full well God had called him. Very graciously God had given him this young devoted friend as a partial recompense, although Philip was unconscious of the fact that he needed any such benefit.

As the weeks went on, he did as he had determined in his heart. He respected Angelena Fairfield as a real Christian lady and he treated her as such. He was astonished more than once at the gift of talents she displayed on numerous occasions. She knew how to meet strangers and make them feel at home. She knew how to handle little children and mend their broken hearts. Philip listened to her prayers at the table and noticed a growing beauty about her face, but he would not allow himself to look twice. He gave himself wholeheartedly to the work assigned to him and he lived with a prayer continually on his lips that God would help him be every inch a man, a true gentleman, but also a man of God.

There was something extraordinary about Philip Spalding, something that made him stand out from other men. He had a pure look on his face that gave him a distinctive appearance. Some men desire a lot of attention because they are so loud and boisterous most of the time. But Philip had a real interesting, respectful sense of humor and he was not overly loud. He attracted attention because he was different from ordinary men, but the difference did not make him appear odd or conceited. The difference was because he had a face with no marks of guilt or sin, no trace of evil thoughts, and no expressions of jealousy.

Angelena could not be blind to this fact. As weeks became months, she was convinced within her own soul that Philip Spalding was an extraordinary young man, and she had not even begun to know him. The real Philip. They had lived under the same roof, and sat at the same table, worshiped together in the same congregation, spoke to each other occasionally, but Philip went his way and she went hers. When the family got together for evening prayer, they prayed for the same things. They laughed at the same funny things the children said and did, and grieved alike over the same concerns at church, but never did Angelena lose her determined choice. She did notice how kind Philip was to the elderly men and women of the congregation and how cheerful he came home after a hard day's work and how patient he was with the Brinton children. She noticed the kind of songs he sung when he was alone, and the kind of books he chose to read. She even noticed the way he always put away his hat and coat, and cleaned off his shoes before coming into the house.

On Sunday evening Philip gave a talk in church. He had spoken many times before, but tonight his face had a special radiance about it that made Angelena hold her breath. He spoke in such a sincere, yet self confident way, so much so, that she twisted the corner of her handkerchief as she listened. He did not look straight at her, but seemed to look at everyone else.

When Angelena got to her room after the service, she closed the door and burst into sudden tears. "Oh," she cried, "If I could only run away and never come back! He makes me tremble."

Many days passed by. More meals were eaten; many prayers were prayed as the weeks passed. One evening Angelena went to the basement to dump the basket in the furnace. Leon and Philip had gone to bed sometime before.

She stopped short. That noise—It must be a mouse. And Angelena did not want to meet and see a mouse!

"Get out of here!" She said as she stamped her foot on the floor and snapped on the light--- and there she saw a man kneeling. She couldn't believe her eyes! It was Philip Spalding praying!

"Oh! I'm so sorry!" Angelena stepped back, her face got white, "Sorry!" She gasped and without dumping the waste-paper basket, she ran upstairs as fast as she could--- trembling with embarrassment.

"OH NO! I WISH I COULD DIE!" He is very kind and I have been so mean! I am not fit to even be his friend!" A letter came for her on Friday.

Angelena,

Father isn't a bit well. Maybe you ought to come home for a while. He didn't say so before, and you know how father is. He knows how you love your work there in Raytown and he doesn't know I am writing this to you, but I thought maybe you could cheer him up a little. It doesn't seem right at all for Father to be down in bed. The doctor came three times this week. I fear it's something serious. I am doing well myself, but of course, rather worn out from loosing sleep. It's been cold. It keeps me busy keeping the fire up too.

Love,
Mother

Angelena gave way to her feelings and cried openly now. Her pretty blue eyes were red and swollen when she came to the table that evening.

The entire Brinton family did their best to sympathize. Philip said nothing, because he did not know for sure what to say.

She was sitting at the desk in the living room writing, when Philip walked past the open door.

"Are you going home, Angelena?" He asked timidly, hardly knowing whether or not to speak.

"Oh," Angelena jumped. She had not heard him coming. She got to her feet and came close to the door. Her lips trembled, and she pressed both hands tight together as if in pain. "I think I shall," she said softly. Her eyes swept the floor and suddenly she looked up and said, "Oh, Philip, before I leave I want to ask you to forgive me for treating you so mean."

"So mean? Angelena!" Philip took a hold of the door frame. "What are you saying?"

"Philip---why, why don't you know---

***

Chapter 12

Angelena looked straight into his eyes. Hers were brimming full with noticeable tears. How could she say what she meant?

"Oh no! You've never been mean, Angelena," said Philip tenderly.

"Oh yes, I have been. I've been mean and horrid and selfish and plain awful!" She cried.

Like when I gave you back that lovely cedar chest and told you twice I felt it wasn't God's will that you should write to me---and---"

"Sweet Angelena," cried Philip, in a hushed voice, "you mean---you mean---?"

"I mean, I never prayed right about it. Oh, I know you'll think I'm selfish and I know, I know I am, but I was afraid."

"You were afraid? Afraid of me?"

"I really don't know how to say it Philip." She looked down and bit her lip. Then she looked up. "I wasn't afraid of you Philip, but afraid of God, I guess."

"Of God? Afraid of God?"

"How can I say it to make you understand?"

"Please--- I need you to say it just once." Philip said, as he looked down into her sad, sad face.

She hesitated. Her confession was hard to share with him.

"I never did truly and sincerely ask God to lead me and teach me." I've realized it for a long time. You---you'll think I'm awful, Philip, I was so afraid He'd tell me---" She swayed back and forth and her voice faltered.

"Tell you what?" He stood a little closer. He could see her neck throb and her hands were trembling.

"That it would be---would be alright to correspond." *At last it was out!*

"And you didn't want to?" Philip stood up very straight and frowned a little.

She shook her head.

"And do you care to tell me why?" he asked. He waited. "Nothing you say will hurt me, Angelena. I'm waiting."

She rubbed the carpet with the toe of her slipper, and drew a deep breath.

"It hurts me though, for it's the truth. For you've always been so pure and good and lived so close to nature, and I've---I've not always been as good as you, and you said God called you to serve when you were only a small boy. Oh, you know what you said, and I couldn't bear to spoil your life.

Spoil my life? Why, Angenela Fairfield!" Philip almost forgot himself in his excitement.

"That's just what I mean, Philip. I want you to be happy, and I wouldn't want to be the one to disappoint you."

"But Angelena," whispered Philip in a serious but tender voice, "would God actually lead a person and let it end in failure? Don't you trust God more than that?"

"See, I told you you'd think I was simply awful, and I've been just exactly that--Awful!"

"But---"

"It's true," she cried. I've never been fair with you. I never even gave you a chance to talk to me and---"

"All because you were afraid you couldn't make me happy? Look at me, Angelena."

"Yes."

"My dear! Make me happy? If you couldn't, then who could? Didn't I try to tell you I'm a better man because of you?"

"Oh, yes."

"And still you were afraid to let God lead you?"

She nodded. A tear fell on her blue dress. Her soft, light brown hair fell around her pretty face in natural waves. "I guess so, Philip. It's the best way I know how to explain myself. Oh, I've been so miserable here of late. I thought---"

"Thought what?"

"Oh, I thought you'd be hating me, despising me, ignoring me, as long as I live and---"

"And you---you cared, Angelena?"

"Yes," she whispered, hanging her head. She felt weak and almost sick.

"Angel!" Philip clasped both of Angelena's hands in his own.

"Oh! She drew back. "What did you call me?"

"Angel," he whispered.

"Don't, don't ever call me that again. I'm not fit to be called such a name after treating you like I have!"

"But, Angelena," came Philip's soft answer, "let me call you that this once, for isn't an angel a messenger of God---a lovely being?"

"But it doesn't fit me" she cried.

"Once a long time ago when I first learned what your name was, I liked to say it over and over to myself; then later on after I wrote you a letter, I called you *Angie* to myself. Then one night, the night after I mailed it---you know, the little chest---I called you Angel, and tonight you made me feel like saying it again---Angle. I couldn't help it. You're just so sweet!

"But you didn't think I was so sweet when I stamped my foot at you in the cellar?"

Peter laughed.

"I thought it was a mouse. Really, Philip, I thought you had gone to bed with little Leon."

"I had. But I felt so bad I wanted to get as far away as I could for a while, so I went down---"

"Far away, how?"

"Far away from you, Angelena!"

"Oh, then I was right when I said you were despising me?"

"No, no. Not at all, dear. Loving you, and not daring to. I was determined I would not let it get me down. I promised God I'd keep my place, and I did give you up. I never expected to share my love to you again if it killed me. I didn't think you cared!"

"Philip, I've been so mean. That's just how I felt. I thought I had spoiled my life for good, and really Philip, the last two weeks I've wanted---"

"You mean you cared that much for me and wouldn't let me know?"

"Why should I? For all I know, maybe you had given that pretty little chest to another girl. You seemed so happy since you came here."

"I've been as happy as it was possible for a man to be without a girl in his life like you-- Angelena! You can never know the sleepless nights I had before I got the victory."

"Oh!" Angelena wrung her hands, "All because of mean 'ole me!"

"Don't grieve dear! The lesson I learned from God is priceless to me. I made a consecration through that experience that I may not have done otherwise. I've trusted God and it has drawn me nearer and closer to Him than ever before, had I not had this experience. Now I see that it was all worth it. No other girl got the chest, Angelena, I never, ever thought of giving it to anyone else. It's gone now."

"Gone?"

"Yes, I'll tell you about it someday if you ever come back and you'll go up on a big cliff with me. Will you do that?"

She wiped tears away. "I hope so".

"Let's sit down. You're tired and we have never talked much have we?"

"Never alone." She sat down beside him.

"I've always wanted to. I love your voice."

She drew a long deep breath and smiled.

"Tell me Angelena, when did you begin to feel that you weren't praying right?"

"It's so long ago, I'm ashamed to tell you, Oh, I haven't even been fit to have such a job here, but if you and God can ever forgive me, I'll be different from now on."

"Well, one day, long ago, Brother Brinton gave me a sermon outline to type for him about how God leads and guides people and yet, I had a deep conviction then that God was leading our lives together. It was plain to me, but I wanted to be sure, and then when I prayed, I could never let myself say "Take my life and guide my thinking", because you'd come before me then, and I thought you needed a girl that has always been an angel."

"Why, Angelena!"

"Well, you seemed to be so extra good and I don't believe that there are men like that in the world."

"Angelena, quit that! No, don't stop me. See what I mean now? I get cantankerous now and then. My mother used to say I show a temper sometimes!"

"I can't imagine that Philip! You always seem so calm, composed and kind."

"I've lived here for three months now, Angelena, and I've never heard you say a cross word to anyone!"

"Now Philip!"

"I haven't!"

"God help me!"

"He does, Angelena, He is helping you right now. It must have been God who told you to speak to me tonight before you go home. How lonely it will be here without you!"

"You'll miss me then?"

"Miss you? Angelena? Miss you? Miss you? --- More than you can imagine!"

"I'll write."

"Write?"

"Yes, I will, Philip."

"And, you won't tell me after a while it is best to quit?"

"Philip, I have been so mean to you! But, I have kept every letter you have ever written to me."

"Kept them---All of them?"

"I did! I have every one of them are up in my trunk."

He looked at her tenderly. "I have kept each and every one of yours too."

"You did?"

"Sure, you were my first love and I never expected to keep--- like I was, at least, until you."

"Someday will you please send me a copy of that sermon outline you typed up?"

"Yes, or I can give it to you before I leave."

"When do you leave?"

"I think, very early Monday morning. I am writing Mother a letter."

"Angelena?"

"Yes?"

"Have you ever wondered why I acted so strangely, when we met at conference?"

"Well, yes I have."

"I wanted to explain myself, but I couldn't."

"How could you, Philip? Oh I hate myself for acting so cold to you. How can you forgive me? I know it's because you are so good. No other man would forgive a girl like me!"

"I can't do otherwise dear; you know, long before I met your parents, I saw them in a dream! They shook hands with me and smiled. The dream was so real. I told Janella about it and she sorta made light of it in a way and I don't blame her. Dreams as a rule are crazy things, but when I met your parents out there, they were exactly like I saw them in my dream. Exactly, and I was so excited, I hardly knew for a time where I was. It was heavenly!"

"I knew I acted silly and stupid and I thought about it all the way home. I was certain that you thought I was---" But Philip, that's all so wonderful now. Oh, if I would have known. I just see now how mean and foolish I was, not to give you a chance to talk to me since---Oh! It's a wonder you don't hate me!"

"I can't ever hate you Angelena, I love you and that's the first time I have ever said it to anyone. Have you ever told anyone you love them?"

"Never, Philip, till right now. I love you and I believe I have loved you from the very first time we met."

"And you're not afraid to love?"

"No, and I am sure about it now."

"And you know it's right before God?"

"I know it is Philip."

"When you were talking in church last Sunday, something happened, inside me. After church I couldn't help it. I went to my room and just cried and cried and cried."

"You cried, because you---"

"Because I loved you Philip, and I thought you---I thought---I thought it was no use because of how horrible I acted and I was sure I had ruined it all. Oh, my faith! I felt so terrible, and I hid it from myself and you---all the while!"

"God bless you Angie."

"OH! I am so happy. I think I'll burst! I never knew I could feel like this!"

"Neither did I."

"Let's kneel here together and thank God for leading us towards and into the truth."

And so, both slipped to their knees and Philip quoted two of his favorite verses. He *knew* he lived by faith. The whole experience was real. He prayed in a clear confident, grateful voice with deep feeling of assurance and gratitude.

***

Chapter 13

"I have something to tell you Sister Brinton," said Angelena the next morning by the kitchen sink. Angelena's eyes sparkled, and she bent forward a little and spoke in a soft, sweet voice. "Philip and I made up last night."

"Made up? Really?"

"Yes, and it is so wonderful!" Angelena was so happy she almost cried.

"I'm glad, dear."

"Are you, Sister Brinton?" Asked Angelena, placing her hand on the woman's arm.

"I am glad for both of you, Angelena, for Philip is such a stalwart man. The longer he is here the more I know it, and he is sincere in all he undertakes. You won't turn him down again, will you?"

Angelena looked Sister Brinton square in the eyes and answered, "I hope not. I have been cruel enough. I've realized it for some time, but I thought I had repented of it too late. It's so wonderful to know he really has forgiven me, and has no bitterness in his heart toward me."

"He's been a real Christian through it all, hasn't he, Angelena?"

"Sister Brinton, I don't deserve this. Already it seems I can pray better. It is terrible to try to be happy and at the same time be unwilling to let God lead you and guide you in everything."

"And you were doing---"

"I know it, Sister Brinton, I was afraid to commit my entire life into God's hands. It's a wonder that you kept me here."

"Well, dear," Answered Sister Brinton softly, "I believe that God has used you in a wonderful way. I have watched you grow steadily in a number of ways, and I believed that if you were really as sincere as you seemed to be, God would help you to not make a mistake when you prayed for the desire of His direct leading in your life. I thought more than once I detected that Philip cared very much, and yet he handled himself so well. Did you know he cared?"

"I wasn't sure because I wouldn't allow myself to think about it, or accept it, even though he told me he cared. By the way I treated him, I couldn't blame him if he never spoke to me again. Pray for me, will you, Sister Brinton?"

"Of course I will, Angelena. I am very happy about this. I think Philip needs a girl just like you."

"How kind of you to say that. I want to prove to be a help to him. I know I am not worthy of a man like Philip Spalding, but I know now that I love him and I need him in my life."

"Well, never marry a man if you feel you can live on without him."

"Is that the test of true love?"

"That's one test, Angelena---Oh, look we're getting company. I'll talk to you more a little later. Do you know yet when you will go home?"

"I'd better go on Monday."

"You'll come back?"

"As far as I know now. I don't know how ill my father is."

***

The following evening Angelena came into the house with her face all aglow. She was trembling with excitement.

"Oh, you never can guess why I am so happy Sister Brinton."

"What now?"

"I just got done talking and praying with Violet Price, and she gave her heart to God."

"Violet Price did?"

"Yes, think of it, Sister Brinton, It my very first person I've really help lead to Christ! It was all so wonderful and I'm so happy I could nearly shout. Just before I go home to see my father, I've had such a blessings with happy things happening to me. It's all too good to be true. Violet was so sad and troubled and insincere and now---"

"Where did you see her?"

"When you were in town she called on the phone and asked me if she could come over for a visit. She wanted to talk with me. I can hardly wait to tell Philip about it. I know it will thrill him as much as it has thrilled me."

"You must give God the glory for this Angelena."

"I know it. And I want to. And do you know, Sister Brinton, it seems that this couldn't have happened to me until I was willing to pray right about me and Philip. Since I've made things right with him the whole world seems different. The sky is bluer and the night isn't as long and dark, and I am going home now with a different, most different feeling. I know for sure that I am in the will of God and can trust Him about the future, entirely and completely, in His hands. Thank God, Sister Brinton, I am so calm and quiet and my soul is so happy over Violet's decision. I know too, and believe that God will do exactly what's best for my father. Thank you, Sister Brinton, and I know that you will be extra kind to Violet after I am gone. I am anxious for her to learn all she can about her new life."

"We'll do everything we can to help her. I think a lot of that girl."

The time came to say good-bye. Angelena's suitcases were on the porch. Angelena drew Sister Brinton close and whispered in her ear.

"If I shouldn't come back, it is because I am getting ready for our wedding."

"God bless you dear," and they hugged each other good-bye.

"Good-bye, Philip," He took her hand in his strong one, "Good-bye Angelena," Nothing was said. It had all been said before. They talked things over and had a complete understanding of each other. Promises had been made and although it was very hard to part, each felt a sweet feeling that was fragrantly wholesome and uplifting to their souls.

Dearest Philip,

Mother has been so good to me. I reached home finding Father better already. Next Sunday is communion day at church. This will be the most blessed one I have ever experienced, for Jesus is nearer and dearer to me, even more than before because I have peace---perfect peace, not just towards God and toward all my fellow men, but toward God because I have allowed you have come into my life. Why has God been so good to me? I cannot do enough for Him. How could I dare refuse to do anything for Him?

In the afternoon there will be a wedding here in our little church. They are a lovely Christian couple and I am sure they will be very happy.

Please tell me all the news of the home and especially about Violet.

Good night, dearest Philip. May the Lord watch over you while we are separated by many miles. God bless you. Your love for me is truly wonderful.

Truly yours,
With love, Angelena

***

Dear Angie,

I can't find words to express my joy, peace and love. With every breath I draw, I thank God for putting me back into your life. We have been having exceptionally good meetings, but I just must tell you that I miss you dreadfully, and I often find my mind on you. It spurs me on. I thank God for the blessing that Brother Brinton asked me to come to Raytown. It has been much help to me in many ways; and with God's blessing of bringing you back into my life---the sweetest, most beautiful girl on earth! That is exactly what you are.

I hope you are having a good time while you are at home but make sure you don't work too hard. Someday, the blessing will come to us when we can work together. Sometime soon, with your parents' consent I am going to take you home with me.

Did you know you left your little New Testament here by the lamp table?

God richly bless you, my precious one, and remember I love you!

Always and forever,
Philip

Six days later another letter came to Angelena which reads:

My Dearest Angie,

I wish you could have been here today to hear Violet tell her experience of how she found Christ. Of course in the end, your name was mentioned. It made me so happy for both of you. Then after a song we all stood while Brother Brinton prayed, and while our heads were bowed, he read the story of

Christ's suffering. It was so impressive to me. I feel so unworthy, and if I had a thousand lives to live, I could never pay Him back for all He has done for me. I want to yield my life more completely into His hands.

Everyone at church asks Sister Brinton if she's heard from you. Every night I pray that God will prepare us for our future home. I know He will lead us about that, too. You are all I need to make my life complete.

I believe that Violet is coming to take your place here. She is a fine girl, and happy in the Lord.

May the angels guard you and keep you from all harm.

All my true love,
Philip

A month later:

My dearest Angie,

Your letters mean so much to me. They are sweet like you. I thank God that I, the least of his servants, have been so wonderfully blessed to have a sweetheart like you. you give me something to live for and to be true to.

The factory has decided to do defense work so I explained my non-resistance position to the boss. He argued with me a while, but when he saw I was determined, he told me to go home. I got another job this morning at Walden's funeral home. I will do anything from sweeping sidewalks to driving a car in a funeral procession. Today I cleaned out a fish pool in the back yard, went to the bank with a bag of money to deposit, helped get a church ready for a funeral, and drove a car. I never thought I'd enjoy a job like this, but it is good experience for me. It helps me meet many kinds of people and it has some kind of softening effect on my whole being.

The other men who work here are hard, and talk plenty rough sometimes when there are no customers around. I hope never to get that way.

Pray for me, "queen of my heart." May the soft breeze of spring sweep in through your window tonight and whisper my love to you.

Lovingly yours,
Philip

Two months later:

My dear Angie,

While I was home over the weekend, I went up on the bluff and stood against a cedar tree and this is what my pencil wrote:

MY ANGIE SO FAIR

My Angie, I love you, my promised one so fair.
Though distance divides us, my heart with you is there.
Your sweet face is before me, framed in soft wavy hair,
Each night when I whisper, your dear name in prayer.

May the Lord draw us closer; fill our hearts with His love.
That our lives may point others, to our Savior above.
May we live for each other, may our hearts beat as one.
Till our work here is ended, and our life race is run.

'Tis hard to be patient, to wait for the time
When the vows will be taken, and you'll truly be mine.
May the Lord send an angel to guard you, sweetheart.
And keep you from danger, while we are apart.

I'm dreaming of a home, which together we'll plan.
Where love holds dominion, when united we'll stand.
I think of the trials, which will be ours to face.
But together we'll meet them, as God gives us grace.

We're bound to have sorrows and pain it is true,
But the joys will be sweeter, as I share them with you.
For Angie, I love you, I love you my dear.
I wish I could whisper those words in your ear.

Four months later:

My dearest Angelena,

Guess what I did yesterday? I bought three bushels of peaches and took them home, and asked the girls to can them, and put half of them aside for us. But they wouldn't hear of it at all. They insisted we must have them all.

I took Leon along home with me. He had a grand time.

One of my brothers told me about a farmer who wants a married man by spring, so I went to see him and talked things over. Angelena, he said he'd build us a new house about one hundred and fifty feet from his big one, if we'd live there and I'd take over the work. The man's name is Henry Monroe, and he is getting too old to take care of it all.

His proposition sounds good, and, Angelena, I am sure we can make it go. He told me to write and ask you what you think, and let him know, because he wants to build before prices go up higher. He said, if I say so, he will pay me by the month, and he will give the highest wages of any farmers' pay. We can have all the fruit we want, all the firewood we need and plant our own garden, milk our own cow, and he'd feed it and ten percent of the eggs that we gather. He has lots of white-faced cattle and lots of hogs.

Mr. Monroe is a Christian man, a member of the church, and I believe you will like him. Let's pray that God will show us what to do. Let me know what you think. I'd give a lot if we could talk things over for just one short hour. In a way it will be hard to leave the church here, yet it seems that God is calling me back to the country for some reason. He knows our future, and He will place us according to His will, for we have asked Him to. I love to tell you once more that I love you.

Philip

***

Chapter 14

"Oh, Mother!" Angelena's blue eyes shone mistily bright in the morning sunshine. She smiled happily, "Let me read Philip's letter out loud; shall I Mother?"

"I would be glad to hear it Angelena," answered her mother, without raising her eyes from the sewing in her lap. Angelena drew a deep breath, and her bosom seemed to swell with joy because it was impossible to seize and hold the lilting rapture which Philip's love had brought to her soul. Angelena had never known anything but quietude and sincerity in her home. Her parents had a way of making her feel secure there. She had been especially confidential and close to her father from babyhood up. And now she felt a sweet closeness with her mother too. Daughters usually do when anticipating doing what Mother's did before.

Angelena wanted to share her happiness with her mother. The past few months at home had given her a new appreciation of all her parents' thoughtfulness. The last time she was at home, she was rather fidgety, and now she was as calm as could be, with a pleasant memory and because of it, her sweet face glowed with health and happiness.

Angelena read the letter---every word. She read with a soft serious tone, mellow and sweet with tender love. "And Mother," added Angelena, walking into her bedroom and returning. "Long ago Philip told me he wrote little poems, when he was up on the big bluff, I told you about it, remember?"

"I think so."

"Listen to this, Mother." In Angelena's hand she had two sheets of paper. She quivered a little. She read slowly, with feeling. "To think he wrote this for me! Isn't it wonderful Mother?" Angelena bent forward and touched her mother lightly on the arm. Her head that was bowed over her sewing and her hair was evenly mingled with bronze and silver. Her head turned, and Angelena knew in her mothers face and eyes, a soft, rich sweetness in her understanding that came with thirty years of happy married life and unselfish living with the only man she ever loved.

"I will keep this as long as I live!"

"Of course you will."

"And now that father is better, don't you think I should go get a job somewhere and get things ready for our future home? If Philip is having peaches canned, I ought to be getting things ready too."

"It would be alright, Angelena. You know we will do all we can for you, and we will do all we can for Jean and Raymond."

"Yes, but I want to feel like I am doing something too. I want to put some of my own ideas into our home with money I have earned."

Angelena was not long in securing a job in the home of wealthy people in Rollins. She worked, she planned, and saved for that little home that was being built on the Henry

Monroe farm. Eagerly he watched for letters which told all about what her promised one was doing---all about the Brinton family, and the members of the church, the recent converts, and the four bedroom house on the grassy slope of country.

***

Angelena caught her breath as she read a letter that came early in October:

Well, it finally came, Angelena, that long-looked-for, dreaded questionnaire. My brother brought it down to me last night. Don't worry, dear. Mr. Monroe may convince the Board that I am needed on the farm. Do you think you could be ready to get married by the first of January? The way the little house is going, I think it will be ready by then. The draft is up to 1,000 by now and my order number is 2544, so you see it will be quite a while before my number is called. So do not worry over this, my dearest.

The next week:

Dearest Angie, the JOY of my heart,

I am thrilled over your suggestion to have a Christmas wedding. I am sure God who has let us this far will lead us on by the hand over rough places, and under clear skies with sunshine of His love streaming through. I drove up again today to see the little house. It's getting ready for us!

Angie, I've just got to make good on that farm. Mr. Monroe expects a lot of me, and I must show him I'm all that he thinks I am. I told him I am bringing the nicest little wife in the entire world, back from Plumville with me. I wrote on my papers that I would be placed on a farm by the first of

January, so I am sure it will be quite some time before I am classified. Do not worry. Just sing that song, "Fear not, for God the Father."

Angie, one time long ago when I was really blue, you led that song in church, and even though I was blue over you, it helped me a lot. So sing it now. Go ahead and make plans for a Christmas wedding. Your last letter was the sweetest message ever sent through the U.S. mail.

I am going to write your father a letter very soon. He's been so kind to me. I don't deserve it all. It sounds to me as if he'll be a real father-in-law. Oh, how I wish my parents---but wishing won't bring them back. I have you now and my soul is satisfied.

Three weeks later:

I thank you for the beautiful birthday gift you sent me. It will be a book we will use together every morning in our family worship. We'll start our home with prayer, dear Angelena, won't we?

I want to take several days off and go home and work up a winter's supply of wood. I wouldn't make a very good provider, would I, and not have plenty of firewood ready? It will be the easiest wood I ever worked up, with a sweet-faced wife like you waiting for me at the kitchen door.

Time is passing. I'll soon be coming for you. What home is there without trials and disappointments, but we will smile at each other, pray, and go on. Do not say such things as you did in your last letter. I know you are not perfect, and if you were I would be afraid of you. I love you for what you are, and long to be, and with God's help I want to be a true man till I die; a Christian husband in every way.

I ordered my wedding suit, a dark blue, and Brother and Sister Brinton helped me select the material. It's being made to order, and I hope you will like it.

Watch the mail Angie. There is something coming to you before long.

***

To mock at love is heathenish and ignorant and base. To wink at love is stupid and shallow and evil-minded. To glare at love is brazen and rude. To despise love is inhuman.

Few are criticized as lovers. Yet how could one wink or mock or judge without mercy if he himself has known love? When one treats lightly the feelings of others it only reveals his utter lack of sense of values for the finest things of life. Many of the realities of life are lived in things, not worked out by hands or machines. There are too many homes set up over a cold, formal pattern. There are too many vows mimicked and they never mean more than the "I do---I will". There are too many parents who plague and tease their own children until that delicate heaven-born instinct for love, like a lustrous nap on velvet, has been pounded and combed till it's stiff and ugly. What is more disgusting, what is more abhorring than loveless love! What is more uplifting than real love? Let the ignorant mock. Let the stupid wink. Let the uncultured glare. As long as the world stands, some will criticize, some will despise, some will envy and many will shake their heads at the lovers. Despite all this, the souls of our youth call out for love. It cannot be denied. It dare not be smothered. It is not a teen-aged craze. It is not a young man's fancy or a lady's wild dream. It is that attribute from God Himself that burns in a person's heart and keeps him strong when his legs give way, and keeps him young when hair turns gray. He whose own love is a sacred thing will likewise esteem that of his neighbor and friend.

The last several letters passed between Philip Spalding and Angelena Fairfield, were sacred and cherished. Each one saved more precious than before. Those long, long weeks dwindled to days---days of great joy, peace and anticipation.

Then two weeks before Christmas, Angelena read these words:

Things are growing steadily worse in the war stricken nations. There are serious thoughts in my heart tonight, and I wish we could talk face to face. God grant that our plans for Christmas day will not need to be broken. The wood work in our little cozy house is all varnished. It's the nicest little house! My suit came today and I like it. I hope you will likewise. You say your dress is almost finished? Angie!

One week before Christmas part of a letter read thus:

"Just five more days until we join hands forever. I looked up the train schedules. Expect me Saturday afternoon at 2:30. You'll meet me, I know. The little house is swept and ready.

The very next day this message followed:

Dearest in all the world to me,

My heart is full tonight. All day, I walked as in a dream, while a dark cloud hid the brightness of the golden sun. I got my classification card today and I am 4E. I talked to Mr. Hedgecock on the Local Board, and he said I could have no deferment. I told him I planned on being married on Christmas day, and had a job on Mr. Monroe's farm. He said,

"Marry if you want to, but the government won't recognize you as having a dependent." So, you see I'm subject to a call any time. Maybe soon, maybe in a year, maybe two. I had to tell you, Angie.

I talked to Mr. Monroe, and he said he wants to hire me, married or single. I love you, but a man must face facts. If you would rather wait than run the risk of marrying a man who might have to go to camp, tell me. It breaks me all up to think our plans might be changed now at the last minute, but I will leave it all for you to decide. I'll come as I had planned on Saturday at 2:30. I'll bring my suit along.

It was God that led us together. It was God who gave us love for each other, and God is still on the throne. I hate to drop this letter in the box with the news it contains, but the powers that be are ordained of God. I'm a man of twenty-seven and our nation is at war, but Roosevelt nor anyone else can keep God's plans from unfolding for us.

When I see your face on Saturday, I will read the answer to this letter in your eyes, before you speak. If your face says, No, God will give me the strength to take it. I know I have done one blundering job of breaking the news to you, but while I am writing, my heart is torn between two forces, love and duty, to you, dear one. I'm sending you a little poem I found the other day.

Step By Step
By Frank J Exley

Child of my life, fear not the unknown morrow,
Dread not the new demand life makes of thee;
Thy ignorance doth hold no cause for sorrow,
Since what thou knowest not, is known to me.
Thou canst not see today the hidden meaning
Of my command, but thou the light shall gain;

Walk on in faith, upon my promise leading,
And AS THOU GOEST, all shall be made plain.
One step thou seest---then go forward, boldly,
One step is far enough for faith so see;
Take that, and thy next duty shall be told thee,
For STEP BY STEP thy Lord is leading thee.
Stand not in fear, thy adversaries counting,
Dare every peril, save to disobey;
Thou shalt march on, all obstacles surmounting,
For I, the strong, WILL OPEN THE WAY.
Wherefore go gladly to the task assigned thee;
Having my promise, needing nothing more
Then just to know, where're the future find thee,
In all thy journeying I go before.

***

Chapter 15

Both Philip Spalding and Angelena Fairfield were only sub-consciously aware of the splendor of that Christmas morning, and of nature's bounty in providing this beautiful new-fallen snow, dressing the earth in pure white. Their eyes saw it all, but each was more aware of the beauty of the other than of anything outside themselves. A queer little lump that ached came into Mr. Fairfield's throat as he sat near the front of the church beside his wife when he watched his baby---his little Angelena---come walking up the aisle in her soft white dress, her blue eyes looking straight ahead, her curling tendrils of light brown hair pinned back from her face.

A quartette was singing softly, yet with expression, "Those Soul's Betrothed In Heaven." Philip met her before the minister who was waiting in front of his sacred desk, and in the presence of all the people, hundreds of them who had learned to love Angelena, they exchanged vows. After only a few fleeting moments, Philip Spalding had his perfect Christmas gift.

A strange thrill of delight swept through Angelena's heart as Philip took her slender hand and slipped it into his bent arm. They turned and walked out slowly, but with steps that were sure, for they had bound themselves together for life, to blend their personalities for whatever God would lead them into.

Philip knew there was something worth-while ahead, something great or small, he knew not, and peace and certitude enveloped his heart. Bravely he looked into his misty future, for that slender feminine hand on his arm, and God was in his heart. From the beginning God made both male and female, the one to complete the other. The feminine mind is more intuitive and the masculine mind more logical. Now there were two personalities, and two temperaments drawn together to make a perfect unity.

As Angelena and Philip stepped out of the double doors, they knew they would soon discover together what the reality of married life could be, as wonderful as their brave hearts had been telling them it would be. Each felt a flow of tender understanding come over them, which bound them together with a great tie that had been pronounced upon them by the minister. How beautiful! The answer to every blessing in life, that's just and pure and true and trusting. Each was full of unspoken thoughts, but there was a communication between them that made no words necessary.

***

Not until they were well down the road towards home, did Angelena look back. "Phil," said Angelena softly, looking up into his glowing face with beaming eyes. "It is so wonderful to be wanted!"

Who could portray that sacred flame of true love which has enriched and strengthened the souls of all who embrace it? Who can understand true love without the joy of the Lord encircling it?

Philip had already learned that many of the little things in life are the things that matter the most. The one who knows love, pure love, know that those inconsequential things really matter. They may be unnoticed by casual observers, but many times it's the little things, acts of tender service to others, especially those closest to us, that mean the most to both of us and are what hold us together.

Back to Angelena's home they drove together through the snow, just thinking, not talking. Mr. and Mrs. Philip Spalding---together at last! The next day Angelena's parents drove them back to their new home. Philip went in ahead and unlocked the door and with strong arms, lifted his bride over the brand-new threshold.

Did Angelena ever fear giving love completely? Why did she first turn him down? He never gave up on her and on God's almighty will for them. Her repentance had been pure. Every morning they fed on a portion of God's word and openly shared their love for God to each other. Work for them was never drudgery. With zest and joy, Angelena washed his overalls and prepared his favorite dishes. With joy and gladness, Angelena gathered eggs and hung out the wash with a prayer on her lips. Just one thing nibbled on her peace of mind sometimes, and that was the thought that Philip might be called on, to go to camp.

With renewing energy and determination, they worked and saved together. Philip was pleased over what his sweet wife would do. He did not expect her to go out with him and dig postholes or drive a tractor. But, it was most remarkable what all her wonderful mother had taught her to do.

Angelena got word that her father was very ill. Philip took her to the train station and she clung to him as he kissed her goodbye.

"Oh, Philip, I'm afraid it is very serious this time!"

"Good Bye dear one. How I wish I could go along, but you know I can't at this time of year."

"You come first now in my life, but if it is really serious, I don't know what I will do without---without him!"

"I will be praying for you both and also your mother, while you are away."

The house was very lonely while Angie was gone. He didn't realize how lonesome he would be. There was a blue gingham apron on the kitchen chair near the stove--- in her haste she had forgotten to put it away.

How chilly and empty the house felt. He would have to read and pray alone. He almost felt as alone as he did up on the cliff by the cedar tree, but not for long, for everywhere he went in the house there were touches of Angelena's personality. These made his heart even grow fonder, and before she was even less than a hundred miles away, his love for her had deepened.

Dearest Philip,

Mother is taking everything beautifully. It helps me so, even though Father is very sick, but he can talk to us and asked why you didn't come along. Philip, it is so wonderful to be bound together in marriage with you. I thought of you traveling here, every inch of the way. God bless and take care of you till I get home. As soon as Father is better, I will come home.

Tenderly,
Angie

Her homecoming was a glad event for both of them. The little place took on a new depth of meaning for both of them because it was where they knew they belonged.

"It is so good to be back," smiled Angelena, looking here and there all at once. "But, Philip, you look tired."

"Well, I stayed out as late as I could, working, because it was so lonesome in here without you, but now since you are back, could you make some of your wonderful fried potatoes---will you?"

"Why wouldn't I?" She smiled.

***

Then there was a death. It was Angelena's father. Philip went home with her to the funeral.

"Philip," whispered Angelena, bending over her father's lifeless body, "he loved you so very much."

Philip put his strong arm around her shoulder. "I am so glad he did," he choked, "I only wish we could have known each other longer. We weep for those we love, and it makes it much easier to have you here with me."

They spent Christmas with Philip's brothers and sister. Janella had set a long table spread with delicious odors and greeted them as they entered the door. Philip carried a sweet baby girl in his arms, wrapped in a snuggly white blanket.

"Who wants to hold Judy?" called Philip, smiling from ear to ear. Everyone did. Mollie got to hold her first, but before the day was over she had been cuddled by all of her aunts and uncles and cousins. Some said she looked like Angie and others claimed she looked more like Phil.

"Well," laughed Angelena with a happy little ripple in her voice that everybody liked to hear, "I hope she turns out to be just like her daddy in every way."

"I quite disagree in my hopes," laughed Philip. "For the first time I beg to differ seriously with my good wife. I hope Judy is like her mother in every way!"

"Now, Philip," said Angelena with a twinkle in her eyes, "I thought I was giving you a complement of the finest kind."

"Thank you, Mrs. Spalding," answered Philip, making a low gracious bow, "but I was putting honor where honor belongs," and at this, the room rang with hearty laughter. They had such good times when they all got together. There was a strong family love between the Spalding children, and Angelena had been accepted into this circle with open arms.

"Jenella," she said with pleasant enthusiasm in her voice, "we've had a lovely day together. It's been such a nice wedding anniversary, and you had such a delicious dinner for us all---she slipped her arm around Janella and drew her up close to her, "after your mother died you must have done a wonderful job of being a big sister and a mother both to Phil and the rest. I think of it every day when Phil is so good and kind in every way, that you deserve a lot of praise."

"Oh no, Angelena," answered Jenella, smiling though her timidity, "only by God's help did I do anything worth mentioning."

"Of course," returned Angelena graciously, "you'd put it that way."

***

"Angie," said Philip one evening in early springtime.

"Put on your coat and bundle up Judy. I want you to go somewhere with me.

"Where, Phil?"

"I'll show you."

They drove down the road in their car, and all the while Angelena was asking questions. Philip just smiled and smiled. He came to a lane and turned abruptly to the right and came to a bridge.

"Who lives here?" Asked Angelena excitedly. "Phil, remember, I never changed my dress—and my hair is all loose---and my---"

"Never mind you hair, Angie, you never looked sweeter to me. Now isn't this a pretty lane? Look at those beautiful trees and wild flowers blooming on both sides."

"And what are all these shrubs along here, Phil?"

"Those are Sumac, my dear."

***

Chapter 16

"In autumn these sumac will be pretty. The leaves will turn scarlet, while some will still be green, and others cluster of red fruit that's poison, like the poison of dogwood. Isn't this a different sort of a lane than any you've ever gone up, Angie?" Philip smiled at her as he asked the question.

"It certainly is, Phil. And who lives here in this little yellow house?" Angelena pointed to her right. Philip drove past the front gate and turned. He was smiling.

"Lets get out and take a look around," Philip stepped on the brake. "No one is living here right now. I heard about this place today through a Mr. Wheeler who came to see Mr. Monroe on business." Philip was opening the door for his wife and reaching for little Judy, he continued, "It's for sale. And the price is a size we can consider. Let's take a look before dark."

Though the doors were locked, they could look in through the windows.

"The house isn't so nice of course as the one we're living in, but now that I know I won't have to go to camp, I'm anxious to get started for ourselves.

"I don't blame you, Phil. Mr. Monroe has been very good to us, but there's nothing like having our own home, I agree. Look, the walls are sorta crooked and dingy, don't you think? But I could just hang pretty wall paper."

Philip was inwardly and outwardly pleased. He was afraid Angelena might shake her wise little head at the lowly place. She was a woman to take thought and consider a thing before deciding, even on small matters. Would she really consider this place? This little house, with a leaning porch and a broken windowpane or two, and a rusty pump?

"Are you interested enough to talk it over with the owner, Angie?" Philip felt like whistling some little happy tune, but he didn't.

"Why yes, Phil," she answered thoughtfully. "We might talk it over and do some careful figuring."

"You're a real sport, Angie," he said, beaming lovingly at her.

"I hope I'm more than that, Phil," she answered.

"You are!" He patted her shoulder.

"Didn't I tell you once I'd live with you in a tent if that was all we could afford?"

Philip laughed.

"Anyway, Phil," she kept on, "It's not the house that keeps me happy; it's the man in the house with me."

"And I am that man," he purred softly, "Oh yes. Oh happy me!"

There was planning to do. There was packing, and measuring, and cleaning, but with dear Jenellas's help and Ronnie's and Hubert's and Angie's it wasn't such an enormous job. Rather, they made a big picnic out if it. You don't always have to wrap sandwiches in waxed paper, and put them in a basket with paper plates, and pretty napkins, and have a thermos jug of iced tea, and olives and celery, and potato chips, and pork and beans out of tin cans, and drive and drive, way off somewhere where there's a rippling brook and nice enough grass, and no cows, no flies, no mosquitoes, just enough shade, and not too many people close by, to have a picnic, and then come to find out you forgot the salt for the celery, or the toothpicks for those who like to pick their teeth, and the can opener, and the pickled eggs all fixed---still in the ice box.

The Spalding's made a picnic out of Philips moving day. Everybody helped, everybody laughed, everybody sang, everybody was glad for Phil and Angie because they were glad.

"Here we go," said Clinton, turning the steering wheel of his jitney--up---up. "What you goina call your place, Phil? Prairie Lawn or Springdale, or Spalding Heights, or what? Got a name for your place?"

Philip laughed and shoved his hat back off his head and scratched it, stretching his brain.

"Well, I---I believe we'll call it "Sumac Lane," he answered at length putting his hat back where it was first.

"Sumac Lane?" Clinton said. "Lane, well, the lane has sumac a-plenty I see, but the beautiful lane isn't what makes the farm, is it?"

Philip laughed.

"This is going to be a different kind," he answered, "different in every way." He laughed again, "Angie and I like to be uh-- let's see, what do you call it-- individualistic?"

Clinton returned it with a laugh.

"For all of that, Phil," he looked back, "here comes Angie now. Do you think she can maneuver a sharp turn with that heavy load?"

"I think so." Philip looked back too. "She knows how to drive better than me. Oh, yes, as I was saying-- what was I saying?"

"You were telling me about your individualized ideas, and the unique way you two like to do things-- Your whole romance was sorta let's say-- different too-- sorta indivi---"

"You think? Philip asked opening the door. "Well, here's another load! We'll have the house all set before noon. I hope Joe gets here with the wieners and potato salad. I'm getting hungry already!"

"Wieners?" Clinton asked. "Look, right over there is a perfect place to build a fire. If I make a fire, can you put a kettle on?"

"Kettle? For what?"

"Coffee."

***

It takes a heap of living in a house to call it a home. Laughing, praying, singing, mistakes, heartaches, heartthrobs, pains, discussions, figuring's, bearings, forbearings, prayers, birthdays, hopes, disappointments, more prayers and lots and lots more, like baby stepping on mother's toes and pulling out drawers, and spilling flour or syrup on the freshly mopped floor, and eating, munching on all kinds of things a child should not be eating and getting some kind of dreadful disease; but all the time Mother not caring because she would rather care for their baby and her precious daddy. The little house at the end of Sumac Lane was a home, not just four walls. It its walls could speak, this story would go on and on;

but walls cannot speak. They just bring precious memories to our hearts.

"Angie," Philip said one evening, across the table, "do you know---pull up a chair and sit down, Judy, apple dumpling, sit down or you'll---No No! that gravy is hot, you'll burn yourself---no darlin, just a minute, put your hands down, like this, till Daddy says the blessing. You know what I'm talking about Judy, we've always done it. That's a nice girl---" Philip asked the blessing.

"What were you going to say, Philip?" Angelena handed the potato dish to him.

"I was going to ask you if you remember a year ago today?"

"A year ago today? What do you mean, Phil? What about a year ago today?"

"I'm sure it was a year ago today that we moved up to Sumac Lane."

"That's right Phil. But then you're always right about things."

"Always?"

"Yes, in the end you are, and you know it!"

"But sometimes---" There was a twinkle in his eye while he took some ham.

"Of course dear, of course dear," she answered smiling sweetly. I can't always see it your way at first, but in the end we always agree, don't we Phil? Because you're always right---aren't you Phil?"

"It's nice of you to say such things, Angie." He took some beans.

"But I'm not joking Phil." Angelena looked very serious about it, "I mean it all. You were right about God meaning for us to be together, and you were right about the dream about my parents, and you were right about going ahead and getting married, and you were right about buying this place."

"Judy dear, sit down---you mustn't crawl out on the table like that---naughty girl, does your daddy do that?" Philip laughed, "And Daddy is right again!"

"When I believe in my heart, I've got the grandest man on earth; can't I tell my children so?"

Philip Spalding caught his breath and held it—remembering---wondering. Wonder, gratitude, and fear struck him all at once. *Could it be that after two years of married life, Angelena truly thought that much of him? Would it? Could it last? When little Judy is big enough to comb her own hair, would Angelena still think that way about him? My God,* breathed Philip, picking up his glass of water. He looked at it a little before he lifted it to his lips. He thought to himself, *Please, please help me to live up to it!*

"Is there something in your glass?" Angelena asked.

"No, why do you ask?"

"You were just looking, so funny, at it just now."

"I was? Say Angie, we ought to have the Brinton's over for supper sometime,"

"Lets do, for sure!"

Brother Chandlers, the senior bishop was standing behind the pulpit that very next Sunday and he was speaking in a very serious tone of voice---low but distinct, so that everyone in the congregation could hear every single word. The back doors of the church were wide open and there was a sweetish smell falling from the leaves and freshly flowered earth, coming in from the open windows. Several dozen cars were parked in the church yard and the October sun was shining down. A slight breeze was coming in and it was one of those days that always make you think back to some childhood experience, when you still went barefooted, even on Sunday, without feeling embarrassed and wondered how it would seem to be grown up and never go barefooted anymore.

Brother Brinton was seated behind the pulpit behind Brother Chandlers and he was looking at Philip Spalding, but Philip was looking at Brother Chandlers.

"The time has come," Brother Chandlers was saying and he put his right hand on the tip of his closed Bible and stepped to the left side of the pulpit, "when we have felt once more the definite leading of the Lord among us. We have called upon Him and have found out that it pays to pray and wait upon the Lord to show us the right way to take us and lead us to truth.

Philip Spalding swallowed hard but he never took his eyes off of Brother Chandlers.

"Two weeks ago, you expressed yourselves freely and honestly as a congregation, as we asked you do. The voice was unanimous. We appreciate this feeling of unity among you all and have told the Bishop and the other brethren know the time has come to ordain a young man out of our own group to an office in the church that deserves prayerful consideration. Now today, your votes have been cast and counted. With praise to the Lord on our lips for his divine guidance, we are ready to announce that God has chosen to this office through you, His people, Brother Philip Spalding. He will be examined this week.

Philip grabbed the edges of the song book in his hand, he felt warm all over---then cold. A bird in a nearby tree twittered a little song and something about that song and that day and the slight, slight breeze coming in across the nearby plowed ground, took him back in memory to a certain day when he was only four. He was sitting up close to Jenella in that very same church building.

Chapter 17

There are outstanding events in most people's lives which mark steps or degrees of advancement. The nomination for the office of deacon by this congregation was to Philip Spalding, such a trusting step in his life's journey, and the momentous occasion made him recall that from a child of four, he felt that the Lord has some special work for him,

For some time after the announcement had been made, Angelena felt like shrinking from it, and a weakness crept over her which she had never felt before.

"But if this is of the Lord, Angie," said Philip that evening, "I'm afraid to say no."

"I know it," answered Angie, drawing a long, deep breath. "Don't ever say no to the leading of the Lord. Only, it gives me such a strange serious feeling. It's not like being chosen to usher or be the chorister."

"That's right Angie; and we'll have to do more praying than ever before. For if God wants me to be a deacon in the church, I want to---" Philip hesitated and looked out over the field beyond the house.

"Want to what?"

"I don't know how to say it," he answered at length. "But it certainly does not make me feel like laughing. You know when we got married I said I wanted to be the best husband a woman would want. Well, I suppose I have come short more than once," he turned and looked her straight in the face. "That's still my ambition, by and with and for the grace of almighty God."

"As far as I am concerned, Phil, you've been exactly that to me."

"You've never been disappointed in me?"

"Disappointed?" Exclaimed Angelena with feeling, "Never!"

"Well," came his answer after some deliberation, "just so the church won't be disappointed in me, I'll do my very best---but only with God's help will I be any good. One can never be too good serving Him!"

"I'd rather hear you talk like that, than doubtfully," added Angelena thoughtfully.

The time of examination and for the ordaining had come. With a meek and submissive spirit, he entered the church building in Raytown where Brother Chandlers and Brother Brinton were waiting for him. Angelena entered with Philip and the expression on her face was calm and trusting. Brother Chandler offered a prayer for the Lord's guidance. Then Brother Brinton asked Philip the first question.

"Philip, do you feel that this voice of the brethren is also a call from God?"

"Yes, I do," answered Philip, very soberly.

"And how can you tell?" Asked Brother Brinton.

Philip hesitated a little, while Angelena looked directly at him.

"It's hard for me so say this," Philip answered at length. "I've never told anyone but Angelena, that I know God had called me to something when I was just four years old. I didn't know what it was for, but the strong impression never left me. But, I'd rather you'd keep it to yourselves. It was and is very sacred to me. Some folks might try to say it was just a childish dream, but it wasn't that. And since this opportunity has fallen to me, I feel it is a call of God, because I hear you both say that all calls come through His people in the church."

"You are right," spoke Brother Chandlers. "And you fully understand all the doctrines and ordinances of the Bible?"

"I think I do."

"Are you in harmony with the interpretations of our church?"

"Yes."

"And do you feel you can work in harmony with the ministers in this conference?"

"I feel I can."

"And, Angelena, will you stand by your husband in this special calling?"

Angelena looked at Brother Brinton and then to Brother Chandlers.

"That is my greatest and only desire."

"May God bless you dear Angelena," said Brother Brinton. You are truly a faithful, consecrated, sympathetic wife, the ideal to one called of God. And Philip, will you be willing to put this divine assignment to work, to put it first in your life, even before your work on your farm?"

"That is my intention, Brother Brinton, Of course I realize that it is easier to say than to do, but with God's help, I'll consecrate all in my power along with Heavenly Father's almighty help, to do what the church expects me to so."

"That is all any man can do, Philip."

"Yes, it is all any man can do, and we must remember that we are all human, and subject to shortcomings of human beings, but we all praise God for your willingness to cooperate, and for your desire to serve the Lord. If nothing prevents, the ordination service will be held a week from Sunday in the afternoon. Are you agreeable to that?"

"As far as I know," answered Philip with faith and humility.

***

It was a beautiful October day just cool enough and just warm enough to be comfortable. The little church in the country was filled with relatives, neighbors, all their most valued loving friends. Some came from far. A young minister from the eastern part of the country spoke after Brother Brinton conducted the devotion. He spoke directly from First Timothy three reading verses eight through thirteen:

8. Likewise must the deacon be grave, not double-tongued, not given too much wine, Not greedy of filthy lucre;
9. Holding the mystery of the faith in a pure conscience.
10. And let these also first be proved; and then let them use the office of a deacon, being found blameless.
11. Even so must their wives be grave, not slanderers, sober, and faithful in all things.
12. Let the deacons be the husband of one wife, ruling their children and their houses well.
13. For they that have used the office of a deacon will purchase to themselves a good degree and a great boldness in faith which is in Jesus Christ.

And he also shared the scripture from James chapter one verse twenty-seven:

"Pure religion and undefiled before God and the Father is this, to visit the fatherless and widows in their affliction, and to keep himself unspotted from the world."

He spoke of using great boldness intertwined with Christ-like attributes that all come from and through devout dedication in the work of the Lord. God has no patience for a man that is not completely dedicated. He spoke for forty minutes and held the congregation spellbound. He finished his remarks by saying, "May God bless this congregation and the lives of both Brother and Sister Spalding."

Angelena, with a wee baby boy in her arms, sat on the front seat with Philip. A snowy white fringed shawl fell over her black dress. She handed the baby to her mother, and knelt beside her husband. Her heart pounded with devotion to him and mostly to her Lord and Savior. Both Brother Brinton and Brother Chandlers placed their hands upon Philip's bowed head and Brother Brinton gave the charge:

1. It shall be your duty to receive and distribute the charities and offerings of the church.
2. To visit the widows and orphans and sick and afflicted and comfort them as best you can.
3. To assist the bishop in the ordinances of the church.
4. To take charge of the services and preach in the absence of the minster.
5. To endeavor to bring about a reconciliation between members of the congregation when difficulties arise.
6. To attend the district conference whenever possible.

After the ordination, nearly everyone present came forward and took Philip by the hand and Angelena too. Many eyes were wet, but few were touched with emotion as deeply as Jenella. Who could describe her mingled feelings of concern and joy over her little brother? Jenella had done well in raising him, but that was the farthest from her thoughts.

It was a quiet evening, that same October day. A heavy shade formed by interlaced boughs, gave the lane a coolness that was invigorating. The sumac leaves of gleaming gold and splotches of bright red and yellow made a riot of colors on either side. They seemed to nod invitingly to Philip and Angelena as they drove slowly toward the little house at the end of Sumac Lane.

"Angie," spoke Philip softly, looking down at her lovingly---only a few words were spoken on the way home---see the sumac?"

"Yes."

"Do you know what I am thinking just now?"

"No," she answered, "Do tell me!"

"I'm thinking that we may have as many different experiences in life as colors on the sumac."

"Maybe so, Phil."

"But you'll stand by me---I mean we'll stand together, won't we, Angie?"

"Of course we will," she answered warmly. "I wouldn't be happy any other way."

"Let's go up to the bluff and talk, if we have time after church."

"Let's make sure we do." She smiled up at him.

"Angel," whispered Philip, beaming down on her. You said I shouldn't anymore."

"Shouldn't what?"

"Call you Angel, but I want to so much just this once, because you will be one forever to me and to our children!"

IF I WERE ENTERING HIGH SCHOOL AGAIN

By Christmas Carol Kauffman, age 31 Hannibal, Missouri
in the Youth's Christian Companion

In a few weeks, I expect to attend the eighth grade graduation exercises of this country
(This is past now, for a number of weeks) because there are four girls and a boy in the group in whom I have a particular interest, and also because I like to live over and over again some of the happy experiences of the past.

Those of you who have recently or years ago, been fortunate enough to complete the requirements for graduation from common school, know that it gives a boy or girl a certain thrill to step forward and receive a diploma with his or her name written on it in elaborate penmanship. You thought it was just about the most wonderful reward you have earned. At least, I thought so. And I was somewhat disappointed at the emotions mingled with commencement week four years later. The thrill was not half so glorious. Not half! It did not seem as though I had accomplished anything so extraordinary.

Then that Junior College diploma, all done up in a leather folder! I didn't feel worthy to accept it as a gift. I don't intend ever to have it framed, and to tell you the truth, I've looked at it only once since I have received it.

I was talking with a doctor recently, a man who has may diplomas, who said, "It's funny, but every time I've had a graduation ceremony, I got less of a thrill out of it, and when I was given a degree," he scratched his head and laughed, "Well, I can't remember that I felt out of the ordinary. But it was really something wonderful when I graduated from the eighth grade!

For you who are finishing your common school education and will receive a diploma for the same, let it be a great day in your life; let it be the happiest experience you've ever had yet (except of course your conversion). I would not wish nor dare to put anything before that or detract from it. Many of you, I know, have already accepted Jesus Christ as your personal, loving Savior. But you have a right to be extra happy on this day, for it is a stepping stone into a more abundant life, a life that from now on is going to be more purposeful. You will soon be men and women.

I believe that many of you young people will be entering high school this fall, and others will probably go to academy or Business College. It is to those of you especially who anticipate entering a public high school, that I write a little message today.

I spent four years in our local high school which had an enrollment at that time of over six hundred. The few suggestions I am going to pass on to you are taken from my very heart. They are my sincere convictions, developed while I was in high school and since.

You may have read Dr. Gordon's essay, "If I Were Twenty-One Again." In his advanced years, learned, a master teacher, preacher, a great thinker, and cultivator of ideals to thousands of Christians, he looked back to his young manhood and said if he could live his life over again, he'd be sure to gear his life by certain definite convictions.

As I think back over my life, I realize that it was at the time I entered high school that I needed most convictions concerning my spiritual, social, and mental attitudes--- something definite to live by and live for. And I tell you confidentially, if I were entering high school again, I'd do some things quite differently and other things more wholeheartedly.

1. I would be more confidential with my parents. I know some mothers and fathers fail to play well their part in the game of confidence, but most parents would greatly appreciate being on intimate terms with their sons and daughters. Too often our chums know more about us than our parents do. This is not right.

John went off to school. He roomed and boarded in town. He went home over the weekend and talked and worked, but had little to say. One day John's father was shocked by the statement he heard John make to a friend. In a few words, John revealed the secret that his Christian experiences had been undermined---shattered by bits of false teaching. John never did get straightened out. His father grieved to the day of his death, when he took John's hand and said, "I had great hopes when I sent you off, John. I thought you were able to stand. I could have helped you, but neither of us took the chance."

No matter where I'd go to school, in my home town, in an adjacent city, or a hundred or thousand miles from home, I'd begin at once by telling my parents everything I do everything I see or hear, everything I believe or don't believe, or doubt or wonder about. For there are invisible forces, both divine and satanic, which surround every single person, no matter what your home teaching has been. And many a man and woman have been lost because he put his confidence in classmates, teachers or chums, rather than with his own parents. Confide in them. They yearn for your trust in them.

2. I'd choose my course with the purpose of being better prepared for Christian service. It is very rare that one at this age (high school) knows what his life work will be; but most of us have ambitions. God made us that way. Our ambitions, however, usually undergo a good many changes. When I was in third grade, I just knew that someday, I'd be a teacher, just like Miss Dickerhoff. I'd comb my hair like she

did and even walk like she did. A few years later, I had forgotten about Miss Dinkerhoff. I knew a lovely nurse that worked in an orphans' home, so that is what I was certain I wanted to grow up and be. And there were other ambitions I sought for before I turned twenty one. Today, I am doing something quite different from any of these previous desires, yet I can see God's hand in what I have chosen to do and can see God's hand in all of it and I am satisfied.

Be ambitious; covet earnestly the best things. Look ahead. Expect great things in the future. Expect to do something great yourself, by and with the help of the Lord and for the church. I'd plan my course, then with that in mind, avoiding such subjects that would detract from my goal in any way. Whatever I'd hope to do, I'd want to do it the very best that anyone ever did, as unto the Lord. If I had an ambition to be a farmer, a mechanic, a contractor, a teacher, a salesman, an office girl, or a nurse, I'd choose my course of studies with the idea of serving Jesus Christ in that vocation. Every state has certain requirements in its curriculum, but also offers a number of electives. Here are a few that any Christian could enjoy: public Speaking, manual and domestic arts, history and music, botany, agriculture or general science. We are not necessarily expected to know at this age what God would have us do someday, but we can work and plan and study toward the end of some kind of Christian service.

3. I'd put forth a greater effort to master the subjects I least enjoyed. It's perfectly natural that certain studies appeal to us more than others, but I found myself spending most of my time on the subjects I reveled in and neglecting the ones I liked least. Was it any wonder that I rather dreaded certain class periods? Now, if I had it to do over, I'd send more time on history, for instance. I give this suggestion because sometime, sooner or later, we have to learn to do some things which are not exactly a pleasure; and it's good that we do. We

might as well smile and go to digging as though we liked to dig. It's part of the life process. None of are able to do exactly what we want to do all of the time.

4. If I were entering high school again, I'd keep a New Testament in my desk where I could lay my hands on it anytime. If I were a boy, I'd carry a small one in my pocket. It's a fine thing for a girl to keep one in her bag. As never before, I need it now to help me, protect me and shield me, to strike at the evil one who will try to shame and deceive and confuse me and make me doubtful. The sword of the Spirit is for our protection. I'd form a habit of reading from the scriptures every day and during study period as possible. Read my scriptures in school? Why not? Most of the students have a magazine or library book to read during noon hours, or when assignments are completed, so why wouldn't it be all right to read a little in heaven's library book? This can easily be done quietly and reverently. We need make no excuse. Let your Bible be a constant reference book. For myself, I found it of immeasurable value during moments of duty.

5. I'd make it known at once that I am a Christian. I would not try to hide the fact until I was found out. I'd rejoice and glory in the fact that I am a child of God, for it's the most honorable name a person can have. This new life is the sweetest experience I've known, so I won't be afraid or ashamed to let others know it. No, it is not necessary to tell everyone I meet. Others can see it and feel it and the Spirit who abides within will testify. But if asked I will confess Christ without hesitancy. Often it is the insincere, the half ashamed and inconsistent Christian who will be ridiculed and scoffed at, rather than the loyal one.

6. And since I am a Mennonite, let me add, that I wouldn't be ashamed to let them know that too. Attending a public school should make me a better, stronger one. If possible, I would read Mennonite history before starting to

school, so that I need make no apologies for my beliefs which seem to differ from many. If I happen to be the only Mennonite in school, God help me to know what I believe, and believe what I know and show my colors (being sure the colors are fast and won't wash out). Few Christians of any denomination are mocked at because of their convictions. But I happen to know a good number of many students who have the finger of any scorn pointed at them by others who make no profession because they are Mennonites on Sunday and not much of anything during the week.

Here is a problem which confronts most Mennonite girls who are starting High School: whether to wear the bonnet. Perhaps some of you don't have any yet, and perhaps some of you have one, but you just can't make yourself wear it. Some of you wear it because your parents insist, and some of you have decided for yourself that you want to. I know exactly how you feel, every one of you, for haven't I gone through this question myself?

Haven't I in my mind argued this question, pro or con many times? But let no one laugh at the girl who is trying to decide. It is not a little matter to her.

If I were entering high school again, I'd wear my bonnet just as I did, and I wouldn't wait until the second day or the second week. I'd wear it the very first day with all sincerity and undisturbed at the fact that I was alone in the decision and a little different. The second day it is easier and the third day still, and very soon I would feel very uncomfortable without it. Many girls, rather than be different, go bareheaded until the snow flies, then wear a tam or Cap. But you know girls it is neither refined nor lady-like to walk the streets bareheaded. I have never found that the wearing of the bonnet kept me from having friends. In fact, some of my warmest high school associates were girls of other denominations and I was never ashamed, except by girls of my own church who hated to be called Mennonites. I could write pages of confessions from students who have and who have not been able to decide to wear the bonnet, nor would I make light of any. I have all kinds of sympathy for the girl at this age. Nine times out of ten, a girl will confess that she can't wear the bonnet because the boys discourage them. I've known Mennonite boys who wouldn't walk on the streets with their own sisters if they wore their bonnets, while these same boys would give undue attention to other girls, even of unquestionable conduct. Be sure to be tidy and conduct yourself becomingly so that your brother need have no reason for being ashamed of you. Dear girls, my heart goes out to you, ---you who are trying to do what the church desires. Be brave, stand alone, if you must, but be true to your own convictions. Be a true Mennonite, if one at all and God will reward you for your faithfulness. I know it. Make it known the first day that you are a true Christian. And boys, this is you also! Help your sisters.

7. If I were entering high school again, I'd try to make more than a classroom acquaintance with my teachers. I'd linger after class once in a while; drop in sometimes for a chat. I may discover some very worthwhile friends who may be of great help to me.

And I would do it for another reason also. It would give me a chance to reveal some of my personal convictions when many, many situations will present themselves. A young student, who can decide apposing currents in all issues, which are a part of every school career, is preparing himself to meet manly and womanly and family fashion issues later in life. I'd let my teachers understand exactly where I stand, what I believe and why in nearly every instance, they will regard my convictions with courtesy. My experience has never been otherwise. However opposition is a good thing and it develops the power to overcome. Therefore I should expect opposition and meet it unafraid.

I cannot conscientiously attend the class parties, but I will have enough respect for my own convictions and for my class to go voluntarily to the sponsor and tell her why, because it would be the courteous thing to do, rather than make no explanation at all, and be called a slacker.

I would try to make more than a classroom acquaintance with my teachers. I know of a very poor girl, who made a friendship with one of her high school teachers, and it has lasted now nearly fifteen years and will become a lifelong sweet acquaintance.

If I were entering high school again, I would not allow my studies to crowd out my regular attendance to the weekly activities of the church, such as prayer meeting, or Bible study class, Sunday school class meetings, and the like. I would not allow my desire or an education to surpass that desire to develop a spiritual life. Oh, boys and girls, right here is where a lot of high school students begin to lose out. I want to make a good grade on the theme, that examination and that notebook. I just can't go to prayer meeting tonight. It's out of the question. Lucy goes, but Lucy is naturally brilliant. She can get her lessons in half the time it requires for me. Excuses! I can remember many. But, if I were a high school student again, I'd never allow my studies to keep me from essential meetings which foster the strengthening of my soul. I'd rather receive a low grade in an examination than receive a zero in my inmost conscience.

8. If I were entering high school again, I'd keep a special notebook a memorandum, a "Thought Life" book which I'd carry with me to every classroom, every lecture, and every church service, and jot down things I wanted to remember, worthwhile remarks, stories, illustrations, impressions, and even personal thoughts. Next to the study of

the Bible, I know of no other habit, which so rivets the heart or an ideal, noble thought life. It keeps the mind alert to catch the unusual, the beautiful, the clever, the powerful, and the clinching remarks. Watch for new ways of saying old things.

Young folks, if you are used to class, and letting things run over and off you like water on a ducks back, wake up! Snap out of it! Start thinking! Think! Listen! Once in every little while, you'll read or hear a few words worth keeping and re-reading. Jot them down in the little notebook. Don't take every remark for granted; reflect and prove all things, hold fast to that which is good.

Some students keep diaries, which are a good record of our lives which will be of greatest importance to us as the years go by. Some day you may be far from home, among strangers, lonely, sad, or have special burdens; you may be misjudged or misunderstood, you may be sick or preparing a talk for some special occasion, or trying to write a card of sympathy, a greeting, a love letter, or what not. Then get out your precious notebook or journal, which will become your bosom friend. I'd like to go back to your age and start a new one.

9. If I were entering high school again, I'd cultivate a friendly disposition. I'd not wait for the other one to make the advances, but go more than halfway to show myself friendly. I would frown less and smile more; be less selfish in my friendships; be slower to criticize and more ready to praise. I would give more consideration to the other person's point of view; I would be quick to help a fellow student; and never laugh at another's blunders or mistakes. He might have the laugh on me very soon. I would give a classmate the benefit of a doubt, and not be bold in stating my personal opinions for the sake of an argument. I would love the unlovely, for they have few enough friends. I'd be a "good sport" in debates and

contests by being a good looser. If I want friends I must make myself worthy.

10. If I were entering high school again, I would spend more time outdoors. I wouldn't stick over my books and become a hothouse plant. I'm young, and happy, and free. I want to get out and play and laugh and run and win. God made me so. A healthy robust body, tingling with energy and vitality will be a great aid in helping a student solve a difficult problem. If that geometry problem is a stubborn one, I'd run out, have fun with the children, or mow the yard, do a task or play a game of tennis with my chum, then go back and try again. A sluggish, lifeless body is often accompanied by a sluggish mind.

11. If I was entering high school again, I'd never, under any circumstances, allow my friendship with the opposite sex to become more than casual, unless that friend is a Christian and one of my own faith. It is so easy to do, and so hard to undo. As one who has been and heard the testimony of some heart-rending disappointments because of such friendships; let me urge you to be on guard. Don't flirt for the fun of it. Boys, don't let the girls fool you and make a fool of you! Some girls are most clever at it.

If I were entering high school again I would be the very best I could be to be worthy of all the blessing that come to those who live their lives as the Lord would have us do.

THE NEXT TRAMP

By Christmas Carol Kauffman, age 35 Hannibal, Missouri
Originally Published October 2, 1938
in the Youth's Christian Companion

"Mamma---Mamma", Little Rosie patted her mother on the arm gently and looked at her with large, blue wondering eyes.

"What matter, Mamma? The child repeated insistently, at the same time climbing up on her mother's lap,

The mother's arms tightened around the fully-headed little girl pressing her soft plump body close to her. Her lips touched the fragrant hair and left a kiss there. The child thought she felt her mother's body tremble and looked up again with wide-open eyes. Straight into her mother's face she looked and whispered half fearfully this time, "What matter, Mamma?" She choked.

They were sitting on a wood box by the east window. A little bird stopped a moment on the window sill, picked up a crumb, and flew away. A shiny tear hung for a moment on the woman's eyelash, and she quickly brushed it away.

"Oh, nothing much, Darling;" the woman tried to smile as she spoke. "The birdie got the crumb, didn't he?"

"Let me put some more out." She made dimples when she said it, for they always came with the faintest smile.

"We can spare a few, Dear;" spoke the mother softly.

A rap at the door put the woman on her feet. She brushed the wrinkles out of her apron and pinned back a stand of loose hair.

An over-grown boy about nineteen stood on the porch. His clothes were tattered and torn, and his shoes were all but through the bottom. His long shabby hair fell around a sad freckled face, and he looked wistfully at the woman behind the screen door, and fumbled with a loose button on his dirty shirt. His forehead was damp with perspiration.

"Could you---"he faltered shifting from one foot to the other; could you---"he ventured again---give a fellow---"

"Something to eat?" The woman inside the door helped him out. The young man nodded, then added quickly, "I'd be willing to do some work for you if you have something I could do."

"Willing to work? Well, not many who stop here offer to do that," the woman smiled. "Several times I've fed men who never even said, 'thank you' I'll give you what I have, but you need not work for it."

"I'd be glad to do something for you, Mam."

"But I have nothing for you to do just now. I'll feed you anyway. Take a seat there." She pointed to a small bench on the porch.

"Get a cup out for Mamma, Rosie dear; and a cookie. We must bake some more today, or the next tramp won't get any."

"What's the matter Mamma?" Rosie looked up in time to see the piece of a tear left on her mother's cheek.

"Oh, he looks so young, Rosie; so young to be tramping and begging---so pitiful and so---wicked, dear."

"But Mamma, he doesn't belong to us."

"If he did, we'd make him stay, wouldn't we, Mamma?"

"I---I guess so---if he'd clean up an' be good."

In a few minutes the hungry boy was eating a simple breakfast, but so---so delicious! Rosie stood watching him through the window.

"Come and play, Rosie" called her mother. "Don't watch him so."

"Why?"

"It isn't polite."

"Why?"

"If you were a tramp---"

"But Mamma, oh; Mamma, I'd never---"she shook her head; "I'd never be one."

"I hope not Honey Girl;" the woman sighed; but we---"

"What Mamma?"

"Sometimes we do the very things we say we never will."

"Did he?"

"I don't know about him, Rosie; some things have turned out like that for me."

"What did?" The mother looked away. The young man wrapped gently on the door.

"Thanks so kindly, Mam."

"You're welcome. And where are you from?"

"Everywhere." He started to leave.

"And where are you going?"

"South."

It was very evident he did not care to confide in this strange woman though she had a motherly face. He seemed to be in a hurry. He looked up the street, then down.

"Thanks so much!" He was off.

"He ate every bit; didn't he Mamma? He was hungry; wasn't he? He is dirty, too; wasn't he? His shoes were full of holes; weren't they? Where will he eat dinner?"

The woman seemed not to hear the child's talk. On she went. "He was thankful; wasn't he? What the matter Mamma?"

"Nothing, Rosie. I'm going to make a batch of cookies, now."

"Before the next tramp comes?"

"You get Susie Doll out and run along and play in the other room."

"If I see one coming, I'll tell him to wait until the cookies are done." Rosie skipped away to play.

The cookies were baked and packed in the jar. Eggless cookies!

"What was that, Rosie?"

"A man threw a paper on the porch."

"Go out and get it."

"What is it Mama?"

"Just another advertisement."

Listlessly the woman opened the pink sheet and read these words: "Sale thrill of the season. Stop at Brown's. Don't tramp all over town to find your bargains. Stop at Brown's first. We carry everything a person needs to make them happy.

The woman dropped the bill in the waste paper basket and sank upon the wood box.

"Everything a person needs to make them happy," she said to herself; everything---to make happy!" She shook her head slowly, "It's a lie---a lie. How dare they print such stuff! All the money in the world couldn't make---"

What's matter, Mama? You look so sad today. Did Daddy?

Rap! Rap! A sweet-looking woman of perhaps forty waited outside. She was humming very, very softly some sacred song the woman inside had heard once before, but where she could not remember.

"Mamma! Mamma! Cried Rosie; "the next tramp has come. Get the cookies out." Rosie peeked through the screen. The woman was in a freshly laundered dress of summery print material like apple blossoms. She bent over and scratched the screen with her finger right where Rosie had her little nose pressed against it.

"Hello, sweetheart---Big Blue Eyes. Is your mama handing out cookies to tramps today?"

Rosie was too dumbfounded to answer. She only stared with her mouth wide open.

"I thought", continued the woman, "I smelled cookies when I came up,"

"But—but you don't look like a tramp---"

"Rosie, you talk too much!"

"How do you do?" The woman outside smiled through the screen. "That's alright little one. You said it, for I'm just a tramp. I'm a stranger here in this wicked world. She looked at the mother. "Your little girl made me feel at home right away, for I take from what she said, that you are in the habit of being kind to tramps and even give them homemade cookies."

But Rosie ventured while she scanned the woman from head to toe. "But you are not dirty and ragged and tired and wicked looking like the other one was."

"Oh," laughed the woman, looking down over herself, as she brushed her dress, "My dress is patched under the arms, for I've had it for three years now, but I try to keep it clean, and I do often get very tired, dear, by nighttime. And once I was very wicked too—and my hair was black and dirty---and I was just an old vagabond, but one day I got acquainted with a tramp, a man who had no home---no place to say---no place to lay his head---no money---but he had a story to tell. I listened to it. The more I heard, the more I wanted to hear. And I found out that one day he was murdered by cruel and fiendish outlaws, just because he loved me and wanted to save a wicked old thing like me!"

"Oh", gasped Rosie "How did he die?" She opened the screen door and asked the lady to come in and sit down for a while. She continued.

"He died a most pitiful, cruel death, just because He loved me and you; everyone. I was guilty of a terrible crime, but this friend of mine came. I met him on one stormy night over in a little town not far from here and he set me free. He did sister, He set me free. He died, when they nailed him on a cross. He gave His life when hundreds of people mocked him and ridiculed him and accused Him of all kinds of things he never did. Think of it! I was the one who deserved to be up on the cross, but because he loved me so he was willing to die in my stead."

"I---I didn't know they did such things these days. I thought Illinois' laws prohibit such a punishment. I never saw anything about it in the papers. How long ago did---"

The woman smiled. A tender light broke out on her face like a strange prayer, for this poor ignorant mother. Could it be she knew so little? All the emotions of that memorial night on which she found the Lord Jesus Christ was precious to her soul and flooded her mind once more. What could she say next? How should she say it? It seemed to her as she sat there, that the momentous hour of her life and had come; and she must, by God's help, meet the situation and answer this newfound neighbor-friend with words chosen by the Holy Ghost, and so she prayed in unuttered words for wisdom. God is the One to communicate with, at the moment of emergency. To embarrass this woman would be heartless. The smile faded, and for a second as she searched the mother's face earnestly--- sincerely. She did seem sincere.

A long time ago, Dear, Long before I met Him---, she smiled tenderly now. Two thousand years ago---."

The other woman blushed. It suddenly dawned upon her.

"But, pardon me," hurriedly spoke the other, "I only accepted this pardon about seven years ago. I was too stupid and blind to see it before---or too proud. What He has done for me, He has done for everyone. He loves everyone as much as he loves me. He paid the price that whosoever, the rich and poor, the white and black, tramp and merchant---"The mother nodded her head.

"You are a Christian too?"

"Oh, no!" Answered Rosie's mother. "I don't profess to be a Christian. I just never heard anyone talk quite like this about the Lord. That's why I didn't understand at first why you called Him a tramp. She blushed and looked down.

"A good tramp---He was. He blessed us and made himself of no reputation He humbled himself and tramped all over the rough hills of Judea to save sinners like me, and that's why I count it a privilege to be a tramp- if you please," and she stroked little Rosie on the arm, "not begging for something to eat, but begging people to read this portion of scripture;" and she handed the mother a small green Gospel of St. John; "I find in my travels, everywhere I go, souls seeking pleasure as I did, and finding it's not what the world offers that makes one happy, but only ruin and death."

"That reminds me of an add thrown on my pouch today, "Brown's Big Sale Thrill."

"Yes, I saw one." Many people fool themselves into believing clothes and furniture and all things to eat makes them happy. But are they happy?"

The woman shook her head. The glint of tear hung in her downcast eye.

"What Matter---Mamma?" Rosie touched her mother's knee. She made no answer.

"Were you ever a Christian?"

"Yes."

"Were you happy in that experience?"

"Yes, while it lasted."

"It did not last long?"

"Several years."

"And would you care to tell what caused you to lose out?"

Silence. More silence. The woman's eyes met. The older one saw in the eyes of the younger the reflection of a soul longing to confide in someone but fearful. Perhaps her confidence had once been betrayed.

"I---I can't now." She looked at Rosie, and the glance was understood. Little ears hear as well as the big ones.

"Go get the lady a cookie, Rosie."

While the child was in the kitchen, the mother said softly, "I---I trusted the wrong tramp once. He made a pretty story---and fell for it."

"You married him?" She nodded. "I can't tell anymore." Rosie was back with the cookie.

"Thank you dear. How delicious! I should be going now. Promise me you'll read the little Gospel. It is glorious and the promises are too. Though all else fails and disappointments, and grieves, and deceives, his never will---never my friend. Will you promise?"

"Yes." Was the sad slow answer.

"May I come back in a few days? I believe you have a real story to tell."

"A sad one." She hung her head. "But---"

"But what?"

"I trusted the wrong tramp once. I was young and easily persuaded. Oh, he said such wonderful things! But---"she shook her head.

"But, dear, the tramp I told you about is all He claims to be. His story is true. No shame. No deceiving. No brags about His love. I'll be seeing you again one of these days. Goodbye and goodbye Big Blue Eyes. This old tramp liked your cookie." Rosie smiled back.

"For her sake, my friend, you cannot afford to turn Him down. My name is Alice Ruebush---and yours?"

"Emily Hill."

Some souls are born into the kingdom of God with small effort and others after long severe anguish. Every force of evil combined its efforts in a desperate struggle against the soul of Emily Hill. Alice Ruebush made many trips to Rosie's home each time making a little more headway.

One winter evening the two women were bending over the body of little Rosie who lay sick with a high fever.

Rosie opened her wild eyes. She was half delirious again.

"When I---I get well---I'm going to be a nice tramp like you. Can I Mamma? Can I?"

"Yes, dear," cried the mother; "And, I'm going to be one too."

THEN GOD SMILED

By Christmas Carol Kauffman age 36 Hannibal, Missouri
Originally published March 26, April 2 and 9, 1939
in the Youth's Christian Companion

"Mother," David spoke as he entered the kitchen. Tall and handsome, he stood in the doorway.

"Yes," answered Mother at the sink.

"Oh, I see you are busy," he apologized as he hesitated.

"Did you want me to press those pants for you?"

"Well--- yes; I did, Mother, if you have time; but---he smiled.

"If you are too busy, maybe Rosetta can do it for me."

"Well, now, if you peel these potatoes, I'll press your pants. How's that?"

Mother Salton looked up with a twinkle in both eyes. She had a way of doing that.

"O.K. I think I can peel potatoes yet. I used to." He laughed. Didn't I?" And so saying, David hung the pants on the back of a chair, took the knife out of his mother's hand, and proceeded to peel a potato.

"Wait a minute, Mother; I'll get the ironing board out for you if you tell me where it is."

"In the bedroom closet, unless Rosetta has it upstairs."

"It isn't in here, called David from the closet.

"Call Rosetta and see ask her if she is using it."

"Rosetta," David's strong voice carried to the farthest corner of the house.

"Yes," came a distant reply.

"Are you using the ironing board?"

"Why, yes; I am. Who wants it?"

"Mother wants to press something. How soon will you be through with it?"

"In a minute," she answered back.

"Whistle, and I'll come up to get it."

"O, K. I'll bring it down though."

"Well, I can come up and get it," he offered.

"No, I'll bring it down. I carried it up."

"Now, Mother, I'll peel the potatoes." He patted her on the back tenderly.

"Well, I can help until she brings the board down." She found another knife in the table drawer. "Don't you have something else to do, Mother. I can do this; I think."

"I can always find plenty to do, but---"she smiled up onto his face. "But---"

"But what?" He looked down at her. He could do that, for David was head and shoulders above his mother.

"I thought it would be fun to peel together once again." Her eyes dropped shyly as she smiled. "You've been away so much. I'm glad you got to come home for Easter. You surely did surprise us."

Although she was not what one would call beautiful, yet, there was a mysterious attractiveness about Mrs. Salton that most people recognized. Her black hair was streaked with gray and fell in pretty waves around her plump face. She looked young for her age.

"I'm glad to be here, Mother. It seems like an age since I was home for Thanksgiving. My! It seems long."

"How long can you stay this time?"

"John said he would stop for me late Sunday night."

"And drive all night long going back?" she asked quickly.

"We almost have to, to make it. Classes take up before noon," he answered. "I wish I could stay longer."

"But won't you be awful tired?" asked the mother anxiously.

"Not very. I won't mind that. I'm just happy to be home so long as I can. You're looking fine." She smiled graciously.

"I feel pretty good. Father isn't so well, sometimes. He works too hard, I think."

"Since I'm gone?" David dropped the knife. His countenance fell.

"I didn't mean it that way, David, He works just as hard as when you were at home. He's just made that way, and---and he worries some."

"Worries?" David had never known his father to worry.

"Are these all to be peeled? He picked up another potato.

"What", she asked. "The potatoes, I mean."

"I think so since we use them so fast. The boys like potato chips in their lunch boxes, and that uses them up pretty fast."

"Does Rosetta help you much?" he asked.

"Well," she hesitated a little. David looked at her closely. He thought he saw a shadow cross her face. "Not so much as I sometimes think she should; but she has her lessons to get, and then she---"

"She what?" Mother did not answer. David waited.

"She what?" he repeated. A step was heard on the stairs.

"You'll probably find out tonight," she spoke softly with concern.

"Well," laughed Rosetta, "got him in the potato pan first thing." Delicate perfume filled the air as she entered. She smelled sweet and fragrant.

"He offered to," smiled Mother as she put up the ironing board. "Did you bring the iron down?"

"That's right; I didn't," Rosetta snapped her finger and heeled around. "I'll get it;" and up the stairs she ran.

"Since when does Rosetta use lipstick?" David asked inquisitively as he faced his mother.

"Just recently." Mother sighed softly, but David heard it just the same.

"And her fingernails!"

"I don't approve of it." Said mother.

"I don't either," said David with a positive voice. "Would she object if I told her so?"

"You could if anyone could. She thinks a lot of you David. She looks up to you."

"Really?" David continued peeling the potatoes in silence. He was thinking, and Mother let him think.

"Here comes the boys. Oh, won't they be surprised to see you here?" She said happily.

"Here's your iron." Rosetta put it on the oven. "Is there something I could do now Mother?" She asked.

"Yes," answered Mother.

"You can set the table." Mother suggested.

"In the dining room?"

"Yes, that would be wonderful."

"No, Mother, no." objected David. "Please set out table in the kitchen. It's so nice out here. You don't need to go to any extra bother, just for me---please."

"Oh, David! David!" both Marvin and Charles said it at the same time. Both scrambled to grab him first. Books and lunch boxes fell to the floor, and for a few minutes no one could hear what the other one said, for laughing and jumping and clapping of hands.

"Is school out already?" asked Marvin, the smaller of the two boys.

"No, no; I'm going back Sunday night. School won't be out for nearly two months yet. Shall I answer the telephone, Mother?"

"Yes, ---No! No, don't---maybe it's Father, and I want you to surprise him."

"Yes, it's Father," Rosetta was at the phone. "He wants to know what you need from town, Mother."

"Tell him we need several loaves of bread and a box of cinnamon."

"Anything else?"

"That's all I can think of now. While I am pressing these pants, David, look in the oven, now and then, after you get those potatoes finished,"

"Beans! How did you happen to have baked beans tonight? My! They smell so good."

"Don't you get baked beans at school?"

"Oh, yes, but they don't taste as good as yours, Mother." He smiled.

"Are they getting too brown?"

"Not to my notion. Did you have a hunch I was coming, Mother?"

"I never thought of such a thing, David. I just happened to fix beans today because the children like them."

"Yes, we all like your delicious beans", laughed Charles, poking David in the back.

"Hurry up with those potatoes and play with us awhile, Davy."

"Well, how about helping me here a little, and we'll soon be done. See? offered David pleasantly. "Many hands make light work."

"Here is one more paring knife," said Mother.

"Are you anxious to go back?" Rosetta asked this as she took the knives and forks from the drawer.

"Yes, I am" answered David; "I like it out there. It's great to go to school. I wish we could both go next year, Rosetta."

"ME go out there?" She lifted her eyebrows in question.

"You'd like it, Rosetta."

"I really don't think so." She shook her head emphatically.

"Yes, you would. Oh, I tell you it has deepened my Christian experience. Don't peel them so thick. Marvin," laughed David teasingly. "That's better. Rosetta, I just wish---"

"Wish what?" She looked at her brother across the table. Her brown eyes shone. She was very, very pretty. Did she know it?

"Well, I really wish you could go sometime. I don't see how Father could ever let us both go, unless we could work our way through or most of it. But I'd be willing to stay home next year and let you go. Sure, I would, I'd find a job around here to help you out."

Rosetta shook her head.

"Oh," gasped Mother at the ironing board. "Burn yourself?"

"No, I just thought of something."

"Something bad? What? What? What?" Now all the children asked the very same question at the same time.

***

A peculiar expression crossed her face. "Something I forgot to tell Father, when he called home before he left town, was to tell him to---"

"It completely slipped my mind."

"Could you call him?" asked David.

136

"He's probably nearly home now. I was to tell him to be sure to stop at Fultons on his way home. Mrs. Fulton called early this afternoon and told me to be sure not to forget to have Father Stop at their place on his way home from town."

Mother and daughter stared at each other. Mother read a dozen questions on the girls face. "That's all I can tell you, Rosetta. I would not know Mrs. Fulton if I saw her. She said it was very important."

"Was she mad, or---or---?" Rosetta wide-eyed.

"It didn't sound like it to me."

"Was she excited?" Asked Rosetta wide-eyed.

"I couldn't tell, Rosetta. I think she meant what she said, however."

"But does Father know where they live?" Asked Rosetta nervously.

"She gave her address," answered Mother.

"Well, why are you so excited, Sis?"

"David, who is Mrs. Fulton?"

"Oh, you don't know her." Quickly spoke Rosetta.

"I don't think you know them David." Answered Mother too.

"They moved to town after Thanksgiving when you were home last."

"SH---"Rosetta waved her hand in objection.

"Interested in Rosetta?" Asked David. The girl blushed.

"That's it!" Charles the bright-eyed boy, nine year old boy pointed his finger at Rosetta teasingly.

"Oh dear!" She waved her hand again. How could you forget?" Rosetta almost cried now.

"Well, the boys here were cutting up so, and David surprised me, so I never thought of it when Father called. Never once."

"Oh dear!" Sighed Rosetta.

"I am very sorry, I forgot. I'll call her and explain just--"

"They don't have a phone. Richard said they don't." Rosetta was fidgety.

"Is his name Richard?" David stood in from of Rosetta and placed one hand on her shoulder, not roughly, not unkindly, not demanding; but tenderly, and brotherly. He looked her straight in the eyes and said, "Is he a good boy, Rosetta?" She nodded.

"Is he a Christian?"

"I don't know. She looked down.

"Then he must not be, Rosetta. Is he in your class?"

She shook her head.

"Where did you meet him?" Rosetta fumbled with her apron pocket. Her hands trembled and her face turned crimson.

"Well, his sister comes to school. Anymore questions?"

She lifted her eyebrows and took a deep breath.

"Not right now, Sis," and he patted her on the shoulder; but after supper you and I are going to have a good visit all to ourselves." He saw a cloud cross over her face, but she tried to hide it. Rosetta tried to smile.

"Aren't you going away?" He asked. She looked shyly into his handsome face when he asked her this.

"Well, I don't know you were going to be home or I would have planned on staying in."

The door opened and in came Father with an egg case full of packages."

"Father!"

"David!" They hugged affectionately.

The Salton family gathered around the kitchen table at six-thirty. There was so much to ask and say and discuss that it was with some delay but they finally all got together at that hour. David had to go upstairs to the boy's room to see their

Christmas presents, then to the barn to help the horses, and to milk the cows, to stop and play with the dog awhile, and to take in some wood. Everything took on a new meaning when David came home from school.

Rosetta anxiously watched the clock. She could see it from her chair at the table. Everyone seemed to eat so long and slow. Would they ever get done? Did the supper really taste as good to all the rest as they said it did? Dear me! The clock struck seven thirty, and Mother still made no effort to leave the table. Rosetta could stand it no longer.

"Father," she said at length, "did Mother tell you what she forgot to---to tell you when you called?"

"Yes," he replied.

"What are you going to do about it?"

"I don't know, unless I make a trip back to town. I thought maybe we could all go in together and stop a few minutes to see Uncle Alfred's, since David's here."

"I can't go," Rosetta shook her head and looked blue.

"Why not?" asked Father.

"Cause I can't." She replied.

"Richard's coming, I'll bet!" Spoke up Charles. Rosetta looked disgusted.

"Call it off," suggested Father quite emphatically. "David isn't here every day. I'm not in favor at all, of this Richard coming here anyway." Rosetta was on the verge of tears now.

"Let's let the dishes set, Mother," suggested Father. "Let's go to town as soon as we can."

"Come on Rosetta, get ready to go along." He could see the resistance written all over her face.

"No. Richard will be here in fifteen minutes. I'll go with him. The rest of you can go; that's a load anyway."

"You'd better go with us, Rosetta." Mother put her hand on Rosetta's arm.

"I'd like to if I hadn't promised."

"You can tell him how it is."

"And how do you suppose that would make him feel anyway?"

The little boy's ran upstairs to get ready. It was always so much fun to go to Uncle Alfred's. Aunt Emma most always had a little candy on hand. Rosetta went up to get ready, too, but not to go see Aunt Emma or Uncle Alfred. Not all the candy in the world or all the aunts and uncles tempt her now. Nervously she watched from her bedroom window. Fifteen minutes passed, twenty minutes and no brown coupe. No Richard came in sight. Father had his car at the gate, and the little boys were getting in.

"Rosetta," called Mother from the stair door, "Come down."

"Is Richard coming tonight?" she asked.

"He said he was." She answered listlessly.

"I hate to leave you here alone, but we ought to go." Mother buttoned her coat.

"Well, just go on; I'm not afraid. He will soon be here." Rosetta's voice quivered.

"I hate to." Mother looked sadder.

"I'll stay here! David spoke now. He stood straight and tall and handsome, hat in hand beside the table. "I'm not going unless Rosetta does." He placed his hat on the table. This statement was so unexpected that Rosetta turned pale. That was the last thing she wanted to have happen.

"Well, I'm staying here." she said in a positive voice.

Mr. and Mrs. Salton and the two small boys went to town.

***

140

David seated himself in a big chair and picked up Father's bible and opened it. Rosetta went upstairs. Fifteen more minutes passed; still no sign of Richard. No car. No knock. All quietness.

"Rosetta," David called at length. He stood at the stair door.

"Yes," came a feeble reply.

"Come down." She came down. What else could she do? Slowly she entered the room where David stood.

"Have you been crying? I beg your pardon. Come over here and sit down, Sis." She obeyed, keeping her eyes mostly on the floor. She fumbled with her handkerchief.

"Are you kept pretty busy with your lessons?" He cleared his throat.

"Pretty busy," she answered.

"Do you like your senior year?"

"Pretty good." The answer came softer than the first.

"Who is your teacher in Sunday-school since Mable moved away?"

"Lila Osbern." She tied her handkerchief in a knot.

"Really? Good teacher, isn't she?"

"Pretty good."

"Do you go regularly?" David asked. The knot got tighter. She shook her head

"You used to." He leaned forward, and then sat down. No answer.

Do you take part in the Young Peoples Programs?" He folded his arms.

"You mean the ones on Sunday nights?"

"Yes." She looked down. "Only once in a while."

"Have you lately?" She shook her head slowly.

"Why not?" She shrugged her shoulders. "Not enough, I guess, Oh, I know I ought to."

"Rosetta," David spoke her name tenderly, so tenderly it made her jump and then slowly relax

"Rosetta." A strange warmness filled her heart. It made her tighten her arms, and then relax slowly. She loved David! What a special loving brother he had been. The warmth filled her heart again, only this time even more prevalent. What a precious brother he has been all these years. The used to play together all over the place. She looked up into his face. Such peace she saw stamped there, she had never seen or felt before. For a moment she forgot about Richard; forgot to wonder why he didn't show up; forgot everything else, but the sincere expression on David's face. It held her fast. She calmly folded her hands in her lap and looked into his face and he also into hers.

"Rosetta, I did not know when I came home today that you were---slipping. I did not know until I saw you.

"Saw me? Well." Her voice fell abruptly,

"No one told me, but you do not look like the same as when I left in November." She smiled faintly too, and looked away.

"I hate to see it Rosetta, but---He went on tenderly, "But, it troubles me a lot. It troubles me that that something---.

Complete silence.

"And, I wonder what kind of boy this "Richard" is. I thought I might meet him tonight, and for some reason he did not come." She shifted in her seat and rubbed the carpet with her shoe.

"Do you really care for him?" She did not answer.

"Does he really care for you?" She could not answer.

"Are there no boys in the church to go with, if you want a friend?"

"Yes."

"But you'd rather ---?"

"Oh, I don't know what I'd rather," she said, "I'm ---
I'd rather be like you if I knew how to get that way." Her eyes
got moist.

"You mean you feel I have a joy you haven't got,
Rosetta?"

"Well, I don't know what to call it, joy or peace or
something I know I haven't got."

"How do you know I have it?"

"Well, I can see it, in your eyes, and I can feel it," Her
voice was louder and steadier.

"You seem to be satisfied and I am not, well, I'm not!"
She almost shouted the words at him and then looked away.

"Are you telling me the truth, Rosetta?"

"Do you think I would lie to you?"

"Oh no!" Surely not! I know you are telling the truth.
I'm glad God brought me home to help you. I was so afraid
maybe we wouldn't get to be alone long enough to talk much.
But I prayed for a chance as soon as I saw you.

"Well, what's wrong with me?" I'm not as different as
the rest of us, am I?"

"Just a little tells a whole lot sometimes." Silence.

It seemed his eyes would pierce her through and
through. She squirmed in her seat.

"You don't like that do you?" She laughed and held out
her hands.

"I don't, Rosetta. I'm sure God doesn't either." He said
no more. He opened the Bible and began to ask her questions
about her spiritual life. She was quite free to answer. On and
on they talked for an hour. He read to her victory verses one
after another and then had her read them herself. She did not
refuse.

"Rosetta," and he once more placed a loving hand on
her shoulder.

"Rosetta," begin all over again, tonight. Give yourself anew to God right now before you go to bed. Let's get down here together and tell the Lord all about it. Tell Him where you began to lose out. Just confess it all. Don't withhold one single thing. Don't be ashamed; we are alone here together. Ask God to bring you peace again and completely fill you with His love and take every speck of pride out of your heart, and help bring you fit to serve Him all the rest of your life.

"Oh, Rosetta, it's simply wonderful what Heavenly Father will do for you if you give him half a chance. You'll be the happiest girl in this state if you'll do that, and I'll be the happiest brother. Won't you do it and make this Easter Sunday the best in your life?"

Tears fell on the floor. The door opened and in came the four Saltons.

"Did Richard Fulton call tonight?" asked Father immediately. He saw Rosetta's tear stained eyes.

"No he didn't," answered David.

Rosetta tried to collect herself and asked, "Did you stop to see what Mrs. Fulton wanted?"

"Yes, I did. She said Richard was called on a job in Tennessee. He had to leave in such a hurry that he didn't even get a chance to call. He left orders with his mother to let you know before tonight. Here's a scarf you left in his car---and —"He hesitated.

"And what?" asked Rosetta.

"Well, she wanted--- to talk to me personally. She said to gently break the news to you personally that he---"Father hesitated again.

"He what, Father?"

"Well, I might as well tell you now dear, now, that he is engaged to a girl in Tennessee, and his mother told us that she thought he never treated you fairy by not telling you so, and she wanted you to know the truth."

"Oh well, I don't care," Rosetta shoulders stayed straight. "I don't care one bit! I'm glad. He's not my kind anyway,"

"Well, praise God!" Mother and Father and David all said it together.

"I'm going to start all over again." She covered her face with her hands.

"Come on over here, Mother and Father," David suggested. Rosetta was crying now, mostly from relief.

David placed six chairs in a circle in the corner of the Salton living room, and together they knelt around the family altar; and when Rosetta finished her prayer God in heaven smiled down upon her, and the joy and peace she longed for became her very own.

Easter Sunday dawned bright and fair, but not brighter than the victory in Rosetta's heart. She smiled at David across the breakfast table; and he knew beyond a shadow of a doubt that it was another answer to their united prayers and God smiled on him, too.

LIBBIE

By Christmas Carol Kauffman, age 36, Hannibal, Missouri
Originally published July 16, 23 and 30 1939
in the Youth's Christian Companion

Lest someone might say, "Simply Fiction," we earmark this story, "An Actual Incident."

-The Editor

"Mom!" Larry's breath came in great bunches. "Oh, Mom, he's talkin' to Fuz---down there by the cellar door."

The woman at the mush pot turned abruptly. From the light of the dim oil lamp hanging above them, Mrs. Maner read terror on the boy's face. Her spoon stopped, and some hot mush spurted on her arm.

"What?" She asked.

Larry stood close and whispered,"Pa's talkin' to Fuz by the cellar door right now." He grabbed his mother's arm frantically.

"Well, what of that, Larry?"

"But, Mom," he pulled at her sleeve. He said, "Yes. I heard it myself."

"Yes, about what? Larry, what's come over you, anyhow?"

"Mom, I heard it. Honest I did." He jumped up and down in a frantic---in a nervous fit. "Fuz and Libbie."

"What about Fuz and Libbie? Boy, are you silly? Libbie is…"

"Mom!" Larry put his face close to Mother's, "Pa told Fuz he could have Libbie to marry."

146

"What?" Mrs. Maner's face turned white. She clutched at her throat.

"I was in the cellar and heard it all. Pa doesn't know I was there. I---I heard Pa tell Fuz he would fix it all up."

"Oh!" Mrs. Maner's face turned white. She clutched at her throat.

"I was in the cellar and heard it all. Pa doesn't know I was there. I---I heard Pa tell Fuz he would fix it all up. He repeated himself again.

"Oh!" Mrs. Maner grabbed the table so that she would not fall.

"And Fuz said if he'd do that for him, he'd get this farm when he dies.

"Who would?"

"Pa would."

"Get this farm? Has Pa gone wild? Oh, Larry, surely you're mistaken somehow. Why Libbie's only a child."

"But I heard Fuz---"

"Momma," a sweet voice from the yard made both mother and son look up.

A slender girl in a pink gingham dress stood on the threshold. Two blonde queues hung from her belt. She had something in her apron pocket.

"You never can guess how many I found tonight," she laughed. Her blue eyes sparkled like stars in the distance. Her dimples faded suddenly.

"Why, Momma, are you---sick?" It was Larry who spoke.

"She had a spell with her nerves."

"A spell? Wait till I put these eggs away and I will help you, Momma dear. Guess, Larry, how many I found." She smiled.

"Ten," he ventured.

"More than that. Maybe next Sunday I can get a doll. I've got three dozen saved up now.

"You're too big to play with dolls, Libbie. Larry gently poked her in the ribs.

Libbie blushed. "Maybe so, but I like dolls anyway; so there."

"That's just all right, Libbie," spoke her mother softly. A tear fell on her dress. She almost staggered over to the mush pot.

"You go sit down, Momma dear. I'll finish the supper. How's come you lit the lamp so early?"

"It's so dark there by the stove."

"Bring in some more wood, Larry; this stove is not hot enough to fry the ham. Is that what you want me to get, Mama?"

"Oh, I don't care---I mean---I guess so." Her head got dizzy.

"I believe I'll sit outside a while." Though it was early March, the day had been very warm.

Men's voices were heard around the corner. Muffled words, followed by a hideous laugh. Mrs. Maner caught her breath. Fuz hobbled toward the porch. He dropped into the chair. His bony fingers brushed the white fuzz on his head.

"Supper ready?" He asked thickly.

"Not quite." Answered Mrs. Maner.

"Libbie getting it?" He looked in the door laughing under his breath.

"Oh, Libbie, he called; you a great, good cook; aren't you?" Libbie did not answer.

The low sinking sun sent fiery streaks all along the western horizon. The sky never tells anyone a lie, to hate, to steal, to kill. Mother Maner looked at the sky and prayed. The Maker of heaven and earth was no foreign personage to her.

"Father of that sun, help us pray. Save Libbie! Oh, keep her! Oh, spare her, my baby, my child; and show Walt his sins."

"Supper is ready Mama."

"Pa isn't up from the barn yet, Libbie. Larry, go call him."

Supper was eaten in painful silence. Mrs. Maner passed everything by. Fuz spilled his drink, and Libbie had to wipe it up.

"That's a girl!" Fuz patted the girl on her shoulder.

"Don't!" she cried.

Libbie cringed. Ever since the Maner's had moved into Pete Spencer's place, Libbie had an uncontrollable horror for this old man. His fuzzy head, his bony fingers his fishy eyes, even his flannel shirt made Libbie shudder. Mr. Maner knew this. Regardless of Libbie's dislike for the owner of the place, regardless of the fact that he ate with the family and spent very little time in his own room as he had agreed to do when they moved in two years ago, regardless of the fact that Libbie and Larry and Mrs. Maner had often begged to move, Mr. Maner would not be persuaded. Fuz tried his patience sometimes to the last degree. Several times Walt was maliciously minded toward his landlord, because he hated him so; but he loved his farm, the hog house, the chicken coop, the tool shed, the house which some day could be remodeled, were all good to look upon. They were good to touch and handle; they would be better still to own. Nell and Prince, and Sally knew Walt's voice. They obeyed him. They tilled old Pete Spencer's ground, but it should be Walt Maner's. It could he Walt Maner's. It shall be Walt Maner's. Walt felt like slapping Fuz for being so awkward at the table. He was always spilling everything or dropping forks, or growling because the meat was fried too hard, or the soup was too hot or the meals not on time. Walt really felt like slapping Fuz now, but the farm stayed his hand.

"None of your impudence, my daughter", snapped Walt. "When Fuz spills anything, you are to wipe it up!"

"I do."

"I mean, you're to be nice about it."

"I was, Pa."

"Remember Mr. Spencer isn't young anymore."

"How are you Fuz?" asked Larry. He asked the old man this once before. He did not answer. Larry repeated the question. His whole body seemed suddenly to break out into a sweat. The bread in his mouth seemed to refuse to go down his throat.

"Fuz?" His voice was loud and clear.

"Huh?"

"How old will you be on your next birthday?" The old man cleared his throat.

"Eighty---eighty six I reckon. There was no mistake. Walt Maner heard the sigh his wife across the table made and he saw Larry place his hand on her knee.

It was nine thirty p.m. Fuz Spencer was in his room asleep, for his snores could be heard all over the small house. Libbie had finished her problems and had fallen asleep on a cot in the corner of the kitchen.

Larry stood before his father tall and straight and handsome.

"Pa," he began; "I heard---"Mr. Maner dropped his paper and looked up.

"I heard what you and Fuz were talking about out there this evening"; he pointed to the cellar door, "and I told Mom,"

"You did?" Mr. Maner did not flinch.

"Well?"

"Were you joking Pa?"

"Joking?" Silence. Mrs. Maner came over and stood beside her son. My, how he looked like his mother.

"You certainly didn't mean it, Walt." The mother's voice almost failed her. She picked up the edge of her apron.

"Mean what?"

"That Libbie would marry Fuz."

"Yes. Mom. I mean exactly that."

"Walt!"

"Now listen people, you know Mr. Spencer has one foot in the grave already. He is failing fast. He likes me better than he does his own children. He told me so. The only way I can get it this property is for Libbie to marry him, so he won't have to make out a will."

"He said he had his will made out."

"Yes; but he said he'd change it if he could have Libbie."

"But Pa, she's only a child. Why, Pa, she's only eleven!" The mother looked across the room to the sleeping child and burst into tears.

"Now, Mom, don't be silly. It's only a matter of a few days and he'll be out of the way and the farm will be ours."

"Ours? --- Ours?" she cried. "Walt, what father would be as low down as to trade a young daughter for a farm?"

"Well, she'd be ours, too."

"But Walt, she's only a child. What would people say? Have you no heart for that dear girl?"

"Heart? What do you mean? She could still live in the same house with us. She wouldn't have to leave you."

"She isn't through school yet."

"Well, what good is school anyway?"

"It's lots of good." Larry put in. "I'll tell you. Pa, it can't be. I won't have it!" Larry's face got red.

"You won't; won't you? Well---well--- we'll see. Libbie is going to marry Fuz so we can have a farm. You folks are too stupid to see I'm doing this for your own good. Do you want me to slave all my life and have nothing to show for it?"

"But what about poor Libbie?" Sobbed the mother frantically; would you make her a slave to that old man? This can't be God's will. I'd rather live in a hut or a tent all my life than---"

The girl on the cot stirred in her sleep. The mother hurried to her side and tenderly stroked her head. "Wake up honey. Come Libbie, let's go to bed."

***

Hurry, Libbie, hurry!" Larry clutched his sister's hand. "Pa's down at the barn. Kiss Mom quickly. We must go."

Snow had been falling since three o'clock that afternoon. The tracts were filled up about as fast as they made them.

"Come!" Larry led the way. "Oh! Oh! God help you!" Cried the mother as she threw her arms around each one and kissed them.

The door closed softly. Fuz was coming from his room. Away they sped to the north as fast as their legs could take them. Behind the hog house Larry had hid their sleds an hour before. Their tracts he had made in the snow were all covered now.

"Here, Libbie, you pull yours, and I'll pull mine. When you get tired, I'll pull you. Keep up sis. We can make it to Sider's Hill by dark, and then we can coast down half a mile at least. Are you cold?"

"Not very. Do you know the way?"

"I think so. Did you hear that?"

"What was it?"

"Pa hollered at one of the horses."

Libbie shivered. "Oh, let's hurry." New terror struck her, and she could run almost as fast as her elder brother.

"Larry, Larry, the creek! How can we ever cross that? It's scarcely frozen over. It only turned cold this morning."

This was a problem Larry had not figured on. The creek was at least two feet deep in some places and was not even covered with a thin coat of ice. Larry removed his shoes and socks and stuffed them in his coat pockets. He rolled his overalls above his knees, and without a word threw his sled across to the other side. Libbie's sled followed, and the next minute she was in his strong arms. He held her tight.

"Oh, Larry, Larry, you'll catch your death of cold!" she sobbed.

"Never mind, Sis. If I only save you, I won't care. I'm too desperate to catch a cold."

"Isn't the water like ice? Oh, Larry, hurry! Here; wipe them off with my apron. Put your shoes on quickly." She tried to help him and in her excitement left her apron lying on the side of the creek.

"Let's climb this hill and coast down. Are you ready? Be careful of that stump yonder. We'll to Sider's Hill now before long."

"How far is it to Aunt Martha's from there, then?"

"About nine miles maybe. We can make it before daylight unless we lose our way."

"It's snowing faster."

"I don't care. Just so it lets up by dark."

On and on they went, sometimes running, sometimes trotting, sometimes walking slowly. The snow was now about six inches deep and made sled-pulling hard. Libbie stopped to catch her breath.

"What if Aunt Martha won't believe us and think we made this up?"

"She will believe us. She's got to."

"Did you hear---"Larry's eyes opened wide, and so did his mouth. Libbie caught her breath. They stood motionless for a minute. "Was that a coyote, Larry?" Libbie's knees shook. They were close to the road now.

"Libbie!" He caught her hand. "It's Gyp. Listen! He's after us. I'll make him go with us. Here he comes."

Over the hill bounded the dog, snow flying all directions around him. He barked to the top of his voice at the sight of the two familiar forms with their sleds. Round and round them he ran barking constantly.

"You..."Larry was about to stroke the dog when suddenly another sound was heard in the near distance which sent his blood through his veins with a sickening sensation.

Libbie knew too, what it was. No need to say. She was too frightened to cry. The crack of a whip, then the mingled sounds of cursing and snorts from a frisky horse! Snow flew high, and in a moment they were overtaken by their pursuer.

"You dirty rascals!" hissed Walt Maner through his teeth. "You're not as smart as you thought you were. Politely turn around and get back home, both of you!"

Neither of them made a move. Walt Maner cracked his whip fiercely, and the horse jumped. "Get up here beside me, Libbe. You are going to obey me and not your fourteen year old brother. He is not running our shanty." And he cracked Larry one across the shoulder.

"Don't!" Screamed Libbie.

"Keep still, or I'll crack you one, Get up here immediately! Larry you can bring yourself and the sleds back home." It was after dark when Libbie came in covered with snow.

"We were at Sider's Mill, Mommie."

"Sh---"

"Tried to run off, eh?" Fuz was angry. His hands trembled.

"She's not going to marry---"

Walt burst in with a furious look in his eyes.

"Not quite smart enough, was she Fuz? I'll fix her tonight!"

"I'll not marry that old man, Pa, and you can't---"

"Not another word out of you, young lady!" And he struck her on the face.

"Where is Larry?" cried Mrs. Maner.

"He's on his way home like a good boy."

"But it's after dark."

"Let it be dark. If he has eyes to run away, he has eyes to see his way home!"

Less than an hour later, Larry came home too. Father and son exchanged no words all evening. Early the next morning Nel was hitched to the buggy.

"Get up Libbie," called Mr. Maner sternly. "Get up at once and put on your best dress. We're going to town."

"What for, Pa?" She asked feebly.

"To get married, of course. The arrangements have already been made. You will be Mrs. Pete Spenser before night."

"My poor, poor child!" exclaimed Mrs. Maner as hot tears filled her eyes. She sank into a chair and cried convulsively. "She's a child, Walt, only a child. You'll pay for this devilish thing!"

Pale and weary from yesterday's experience, Libbie refused to eat breakfast. At the point of a revolver, she was forced to get into the buggy beside old Fuz.

"Oh, Larry," cried the Mother. "Come and let us plead to the Lord and beg for mercy! Let us beg God to stop this in some way. This is the awfulest, awfulest, thing I ever heard of! It will kill me. My precious Libbie! My baby!" She dropped to her knees beside the wood bin with Larry beside her.

Libbie cried all the way to Stockton and then would burst out loud in spite of that old man by her side. She wished she could fall out of the buggy and be killed before they got to town.

"Dry those tears now Libbie", spoke her father roughly. "We will soon be in town. You'll fix up that will today, too?" This he said to the old man smiling graciously at him.

"I'll fix it up, Mr. Maner. You bet I will today, sir."

Libbie shivered. The swing on the maple tree beside the house seemed to change into gallows, but it would not hang her. The snow covered lawn where she and Larry had played tag seemed suddenly to become one large graveyard, but she could not be buried there. Every board in the house, every shingle, every nail, seemed to cry out, Prison, Prison! And she could not escape. She caught her breath. Nel stopped.

"This is the place." On a wooden sign in front of the house were these words. "Marriages Preformed Here."

Fuz could not get out of the buggy by himself. Walt Maner helped him out and up to the door.

"I'll wait out here in the buggy." And like a sneaking dog, Walt hurried back to the buggy. The Justice of the Peace was a young father, about thirty- five years of age. He was humming softly, when this couple knocked.

"Mornin', "Fuz answered.

"What can I do for you?"

"We want to get married." Fuz wiped his face nervously.

"To this---to this girl? Libbie burst into tears. He nodded.

"Her father gave his consent," He pointed out to the buggy with his cane.

"But Mommie didn't." sobbed Libbie; I don't want to marry him. I hate him. I don't care. I do!"

Fuz Spenser coughed.

"I'll fix…"he did not finish his sentence.

"I wouldn't grant you a license at any price, said the Justice Of The Peace. He placed a strong hand on Libbie's shoulder. "How old are you, little sister?"

"Eleven, sir."

"You go back home to your mother, Honey. You have plenty of time to think about getting married. You have more sense than your father. There is something wrong here, something very wrong. I have a notion to report him. Who is your father?"

"Walt Maner."

"And your name?

"Libbie."

"Let's go Libbie." Said her father.

The girl looked back at the Justice Of The Peace, and smiled a big "thank you"

"Isn't she pretty Arthur?" His wife in the adjoining room stepped in.

"Arthur, wasn't she pitiful? Oh, that poor pretty little girl!"

"Did you ever hear of anything so shameful Mary? It's a crime."

Walt helped Fuz into the buggy. "Didn't it work, Fuz?" Walt's voice was dry and husky.

"Wha?" Was the disgusted answer.

They drove to the center of town. Stocktown was not a large place, but it was the county seat. Walt stopped the horse in front of the courthouse.

"The judge's office was right to the left, in there. He's a heavy set man with a black mustache."

The judge was busy, and a woman came to the window. "You wish to marry this child?" She demanded.

"Yes."

"How old are you?" She pointed her pencil to Libbie and frowned.

"Eleven, Ma'am."

"Just a minute. Mr. Judge; please come to the desk." He removed his glasses and scrutinized the strange pair.

"Would you grant a marriage license to these people?"

"What! Is this girl your granddaughter?"

"She's no kin."

"How old are you little girl?" She blushed. Must she tell again?

"I'm eleven years old," Her head dropped.

"I'll not grant you a license nor marry you, or to marry anyone else in this town who would do a dastardly thing like that. If that child needs a home, I'll find a good one for her. If you need a home, I will find one for you, too.'

"Let's go Libbie. Say; you sit over there on the seat. I'm---I'm going over here a little to talk to---this man, Libbie." She obeyed.

"The judge was still standing at the window. He wrapped on the desk with his pencil after she walked away. Libbie looked up. He motioned for her to come over.

"What's your name, child?"

"Libbie Maner."

"Where do you live?"

"Five miles out."

"Who with?"

"My parents."

"Do they know this?"

"Yes; my father---he forced me to." Her lip trembled.

"Why?"

"So he could get this farm."

"I see." He stroked his mustache. "For a farm---I could have him arrested. You ought to be in school. Do you like school?"

"Yes sir, I do."

"How far are you?"

"Fifth grade, sir."

"God bless you, child." He shook her slender little hand. "Brown is the name. If you ever need help, you can always come to me."

"Thank you, Mr. Brown." For the second time that morning Libbie smiled to a man.

It was ten o-clock when Fuz and Libbie walked down those cement steps to the buggy.

"Fixed up?" Asked Walt Maner. "Wouldn't the judge do it either?"

"Nah."

"Well, we'll find one who will. You two will be married today. It's five miles to Welton."

"Were not going over there, are we, Pa?" Cried Libbie now with a new fear.

"Were going." Walt Maner set his jaw, and off to Welton they went as fast as Nel could take them. Not a word was spoken all the way. But, Libbie could hear her father's breath, fast and hard, and his fists clenched the lines fiercely.

"The Justice of Peace lives in that gray stone house. I'm going in first and talk with him."

In about ten minutes he came out to the buggy chuckling triumphantly. "Go in, folks; I fixed it up for you."

"Oh!" Libbie almost fell out of the buggy. She felt sick and dizzy.

Inside and elderly man met them and shook hands. He had been drinking. "So you wish to be married?" Libbie shook her head.

"That's fine; come in Susie. You are to be a witness. Do you, Mr. Spencer, take this woman by your side to be your wedded wife?"--- And so on.

"Yes", answered Fuz.

"And do you take this man by your side to be your wedded husband?"

159

"NO!" answered Libbie, firmly.

The justice seemed not to hear. He pronounced them man and wife; and they left the stone house. Libbie heard him laugh and say, "Poor fools." The clock struck twelve.

"Miss Susie. I must go to the post office now." Said the Justice, as he put the bills in his pocket. "That was quickly done for a little extra spending money. But, don't you tell my wife. I'll bring you a little present when I come back. Here, help me put on my coat." He put on his hat and left the house. The man slipped on the third step which happened to be icy, and fell backwards hitting his head. Walt rushed to his assistance. Susie came out screaming, and the man's wife from the kitchen, came out with dough on her hands. One gasp and he was gone.

"His neck is broken; I believe," Walt Maner said this. He helped carry him into the house and stayed until the doctor arrived.

"He went against the will of God, Pa." ventured Libbie as they drove away.

"I said, NO," but he acted like he did not hear me. He did. I know he did, and I am still little Libbie Maner."

"You're Mrs. Spencer now, little gal." Said the old man patting her on the arm.

"NO, I'm NOT!" I'm going back to school, and I'll not---"

"Sh! Remember what I have in my pocket here."

"Remember that broken neck too, Pa."

"Wasn't that quick? My, my," and Fuz shook his head.

Libbie buttoned her coat up around her neck and closed her eyes.

***

"Momie!" Libby flew into her mother's arms.

"Tell me everything; everything dear."

"I will, I am as weak as a rag and I really need a glass of milk."

"Poor child." She brought her a glass of cold refreshing milk. Exactly what she needed.

Mother sat on one side and Larry on the other, while she related all that had happened after they left that very morning. Sometimes they all laughed and sometimes they cried. Sometimes they both kissed Libbie.

Momie, I'm not a wife; am I?"

"I---I don't know dear, I think not."

"Oh, Libbie," called Fuz from his room; Please, Libbie, come here,"

"NO!"

"You go!" demanded her father angrily.

"NEVER! I'll obey as far as I can, Pa. But, you'll kill me before I put a foot in that awful man's room. I'm going to stay right her with Momie."

"Come here Libbie!" he shouted louder.

"What do you want Mr. Spencer." Libby and her mother went to the door.

"I want Libbie to come here."

"She is not coming, Mr. Spencer. Libbie is a child and she will stay right by my side, constantly as long as you live."

He did not come to the table for supper. He said he was ill. Walt Maner sincerely hoped for the wrong.

A week later a well-dressed man knocked on the door. Mrs. Maner answered.

"How do you do? Madam. Is Mr. Maner here?"

"Yes, Sir; here he is." I am Mr. Spencer's son from Osbern. I want to have my family on the place here as soon as possible, since my father has given me the deed to the place here, and---"

"The deed?" shouted Mr. Maner.

"Yes, Sir; the deed. We just got things set up last week. See?"

"Last week?" Walt Maner's face got ashy, and he grabbed the casing for support.

"Yes, Sir. I just wanted to notify you to vacate as soon as possible so I can get the family out of here in time to begin the spring work."

Now, Walt got white with anger. "That hound!" he muttered.

"Who?"

"Your father, I mean. He lied to me. He deceived me! His wife was to get this place."

"His wife?" She has been dead for fifteen years.

"His wife is my daughter!" And Walt pointed to Libbie.

"That girl there? My father's wife?"

"Where is he?"

"In his room, I reckon."

Homer Spencer found his aged father in bed. They talked behind closed doors for several hours.

"Pa," spoke Mrs. Maner affectionately. "Don't pace the floor like that. It's all coming to you, so it is, Pa. As you sow, so shall you reap. It wasn't right. God couldn't bless such actions. Can't you see it now? I often have to wonder how you ever escaped without breaking your neck. I've been praying for you to repent before it's forever too late. I'm glad we have to move. Let's go tomorrow. Every inch of this place is like a nightmare to me." She hesitated.

"Me too, now. I believe Fuz is losing his mind. I saw him have a gun today. He said he was going to kill her."

"Libbie?" He nodded.

"Let's move tomorrow, Pa. Please?"

"If we can find a place."

Walt was up early helping his wife pack.

162

"I'm going to have Fuz arrested."

"No, Walt, I am. Libbie is going to town with me tomorrow to testify against him. Let it go, Walt."

"I will not let it go. He lied to me. He deceived me."

"Let's go to Aunt Martha's until we find a place," suggested Libbie.

That is exactly what they did. By noon the house was empty except for one room. Mrs. Maner went in and said good-bye to him. "And, God bless you, Mr. Spencer, and help you prepare for your long journey." He made no answer. He looked at her like a wounded cat. Hatred and pity were mingled in those fishy eyes.

"Do you think you can make it alone here for a few days, Mr. Spencer?

"I don't know. I don't care if I do or not. I don't care about anything."

Go in, Libbie, and tell Mr. Brown, the Judge, what I told you," Said Walt Maner.

He smiled tenderly. "Listen, Child, I could put that old man behind bars for life if I wanted to; but if I did, your father would go there too."

"Really? Oh!"

"Really, I mean it. He deserves nothing less. You go and tell him what I said. He wasn't man enough to come in here with you; was he?"

A child's love often puts a parent's love to shame. Libbie's father behind bars! She could not bear to think of it.

"What did he say?"

"Oh, Pa," began Libbie. Listen, Pa, I love you: I love you. It would be an awful thing to go to prison. Don't you pity old Fuz at all, Let him die at home. He can't live long anymore, anyway.

"But he threatened to kill you!

"Didn't you once too?"

Walt colored up. He dropped his head. In less than a week, the Maner's were living on a small place seven miles south of Stocktown. It was a cozy small place, close to a school house and close to a white little church too.

"Did you hear the news?" Asked Walt Maner at the dinner table. "Fuz died last night. Bill Smith told me in town this morning.

"Poor Fuz," spoke Mrs. Maner softly. I wonder if he was ready to go."

One morning in late April, Mother Maner did not get up. Libbie called her, but she did not answer.

"Momie! Oh, Momie! She cried. "Momie, wake up!"

But she did not wake up in this world. They called for Aunt Martha to come at once. No two children ever cried harder than Libbie and Larry did that morning.

"Libbie," Walt folded his daughter to his chest and cried openly. "Oh, Libbie, forgive me for all my meanness. I've been a wicked, wicked man. I see it now. "I've killed Momie." He sobbed. "It's all my fault. God forgive me!" And together they knelt beside the sleeping woman, whose face was a picture of perfect peace; and they stayed there until Walt Maner's face, too showed peace of salvation that comes through the forgiveness of sins.

CRACKERS AND CHEESE

By Christmas Carol Kauffman, age 39 Hannibal, Missouri
Originally published November 12, 1939
in the Youth's Christian Companion

"Reggie." There was a far-away echo in Mrs. Dunkin's voice, as if it came over a distant hill, but she was close enough for Reggie to reach out and touch her. The uplifted biscuit dropped suddenly.

"Yes," came his soft answer; "what is it, Mother?" He waited a full minute before she began. She sipped her coffee, and then said abruptly, "We'd better find a cheaper house, Reggie."

She expected him to answer, but he did not. Reggie was so unexpected in his attitudes at times.

"The doctor said today that it may be a month yet before Father gets out, and---and God only knows how soon he'll be able to go back to work again." Reggie nodded.

"I haven't talked this over with him," she continued, "but I'm sure he must lay there and wonder how we're ever going to make ends meet. Reggie, you see we could live just as happily in a smaller house," She hesitated and looked her son full in the face.

"Don't you think so Reggie? Don't you think?" She repeated.

"Certainly, certainly, Mother; I do. I've been thinking of this very thing but hated to mention it. We've lived here for ten years now, an'----"

"It's twelve," she corrected.

"Is it twelve? Well, so long that it seems like home at least, and I know you'd hate to leave your garden, and Mrs.

Porter over here, and Grandma Wilcox over there, and the plum trees, an'---"

"Oh, yes, but Reggie, I think of poor father!" Her eyes filled with tears.

"I know, Mother; we could find a cheaper place now that Katherine is married and moved all of her stuff out; we don't need a big---"

"Hi, Reggie!" Dick Matson stepped on to the back porch.

"Hi, Dick. Come on in."

"No thanks. I'm going along to Parkville."

"Why?"

"Just riding around. Come along."

"I can't tonight,"

"Come on Reg."

"I want to go to the hospital to see our father."

"Worse?"

"No, but I want to go see him."

"So long then."

"Be good."

Dick laughed over his shoulder. "Can't" he called back.

"I wish you'd be looking around, Reggie, for some clean little house for less rent than we pay here."

Reggie Dunkin suddenly felt his responsibility for his parents, now that Katherine was married and living four hundred miles away. Peggie, Reggie's twin sister died so long ago, he could scarcely remember anything but a certain little red calico dress she wore so much. If she were living, she could bear her part with him. But she wasn't. Reggie was not one of these dreamy sorts of fellows that live mostly on imagination and good looks. He was a practical "face to face" facts boy. He had just finished his sophomore year in high school. One would hardly call him handsome or dashingly popular, for many of the activities of high school were just menus for Reggie Dunkin. He was popular however in the church, among both young and old, for he had a genuine sincerity about him, and a friendly disposition that wasn't exactly ordinary. Now his father lay in the hospital recovering from an automobile accident. Reggie straightened his shoulders and said, "I'm going to try to find a place close to the mill, so when Father does feel able to back to work, he won't have to walk so far—then. He smiled.

"I'm going to start working tomorrow, Mother."

"You are?" she asked with surprise. "And who for?"

"For Mr. Turner."

"What Mr. Turner?"

"Mr. Arthur Turner, the grocer. Mother, don't act so shocked. Didn't I tell you I was looking for a job?"

"Well, yes, but---"

"But what, Mother?" Laughed Reggie.

"Didn't you have any faith that I would?"

"Well, --- well," she fumbled with her coffee handle. "That's such a nice place, and you're only sixteen, an'---"

Reggie looked a little hurt. Didn't his mother think he could handle it? Was he really just a boy-of-a-man yet? His face got red and he drew a deep breath.

Mother Dunkin saw her mistake and quickly attempted to remedy it by saying, "But you can do it, Reggie. I'm sure you can since you are always true and honest, and never stop doing anything that isn't Christian."

"I don't intend to, Mother."

Eight days later, Mrs. Dunkin and Reggie were taking down curtains and packing dishes.

"And Reggie, our rugs and linoleums will just fit, too." Mother chuckled, "and there's the nicest little old lady next door who came over today and introduced herself, and who is she but, Mr. Turner's mother-in-law!?"

"Well!" And she has the prettiest quilt in a frame. And she made me go over and look at it; and then she gave me a glass of the best lemonade.

"And what do you suppose, Reggie? She lived just two miles from my home when she was a child. And she said she'd like to come along to church with us sometimes, too."

On and on his mother talked, half laughing and half singing, at times.

"Then it won't be so hard for you after all to pull up and leave the old home here, and move into a little house?"

"You couldn't have found a cuter little place, Reggie. And, haven't you noticed a decided improvement in Father since we told him? You know, Reggie, I believe he worried about how we could come up with the payments."

"Yes, since I am working, too, he feels better", added Reggie.

"That's the truth," agreed Mother Dunkin.

"Oh, really, God's been so good to us, Reggie. Father could have been hurt much worse. The doctor said yesterday he might come home in ten days."

"Oh!"

"Yes; he did, Reggie. Oh!"

The joy in the woman's heart could not be hid. Well, what was the use of hiding it or trying to? She just beamed as she flew around the house getting things ready to move.

"I saw your boss this evening." Reggie was standing at his father's bedside in the long hospital ward. "He came in to see Mr. Penderson over there,"---he pointed to a man several beds down the line---"and stopped to speak to me."

"That was nice." Reggie said.

"He said you were making good in the store, Son, I like to hear such things."

"So do I Father. I would certainly hate to hear the opposite. Something happened today. I didn't know what to do."

"What's that my boy?" Mr. Dunkin raised his head and touched Reggie on the arm.

"Well, a nicely dressed man about fifty years old came into the store and asked for a box of crackers and a dimes worth of cheese. He said he was in a hurry and had to catch a train. His bill was twenty cents, and he handed me a quarter. I handed him his crackers and cheese and went to get the change; when I turned around, he was going out the door. I ran after him as fast as I could, and by the time I got to the door, he was running down the street with a suitcase in one hand and the sack in the other. I called him, but he just went on. I could hear the train. Everybody was looking at him, and laughing, for it did look funny. There I stood watching him."

"And then what?" His father asked.

"Then I didn't know what to do with the nickel. It wasn't mine, and it wasn't Mr. Turners, and I didn't know the man's name or where he lives so then ---!"

"And then what?"

"What did Mr. Turner say?"

"He said I should keep the nickel and to forget about it."

"Well?"

"But Father, it's really not mine you see." Reggie's face looked a little puzzled.

"Give it to the Lord."

"I don't know if He'd want it."

"Under the circumstances I believe He'd accept it." And at this Reggie's father had to smile because of his honest, tenderhearted son.

"Father, are you soon going to be up and out and moving around?"

"I hope so Reggie."

In two months Reggie received a raise in his pay. It was the most acceptable surprise, too. He was doing his best to help his parents get the necessities of life. His father would soon be able to go back to work, and then it would be time for school to open. But could he go? Would it be right for him even to consider going to high school with a large hospital bill charged to Martin Dunkin? It was no small problem to Reggie, for he was eager to continue his schooling, as eager as a boy ever was. What would George, and Sam, and Fred, do under like circumstances? They would likely go. He prayed earnestly about this many times.

"You go back to school, Reggie", said his Father.

"But Father", put in Reggie, How can I do it with you still recovering?"

"I don't know, Son, but God our Heavenly Father will make a way. We both pray to him every day."

Reggie could see that Mother looked anxious. These past months had been anxious ones for her since the day of the accident. Her hair was gray now where it had not been, and he noticed his father's hands tremble.

He remembers the night the minster preached on "Sacrifices." It seemed every word went straight home to Reggie. He thought he once saw a tear trickle down his father's cheek. Prayer is the soul's sincere desire, and Reggie did desire to do God's will. Every Christian has had some soul struggles with "want to" and "ought to." Now Reggie Dunkin did want to go to school! Oh, how he wanted to!

He stayed on his knees for thirty minutes. The perspiration stood out on his face in great drops. He cried but no one saw except the angels of the Lord. When Reggie finally went to bed, he immediately fell into a peaceful sleep.

"I've given it up," he said at the breakfast table the next morning.

"Given up what?" Both Father and Mother asked at once.

"Going to school this year, Father, I'm going to keep my job and help you out this winter. It's too much on you to be here without my help."

"That's what you've really decided, my boy?" His lips quivered.

"Yes; I don't want to go this year because I know I ought not to. My duty to you comes first. It is all settled now."

A well dressed man stood at the counter waiting. Reggie was busy arranging cans of corn on the shelf.

"Busy, Lad?" Reggie looked up.

"Not too busy, Sir." He caught his breath. A queer but pleasant sensation crept over his body, starting at his toes coming upward. The face was strangely familiar and kind.

"Are---are you---?" Reggie looked over the counter and the man look straight in his eyes.

"Aren't you the man who gave me a quarter and your bill was twenty cents?"

"Let me see. He took his hat off and scratched his head.

"I'm sure you are the man who had to hurry to catch the train, and ran down the street, and I tried to stop you. Say---and Reggie reached into his pocket and drew out a coin---"here is your change, Sir. I've waited a long time to give it to you, Sir, I kept it for you."

"You mean my boy, that you never spent it?"

"No, Sir, I never did. Mr. Turner said I could buy candy with it---and he laughed---"but I'm not so strong on candy, and so here it is, Sir. It's not mine. You gave me a quarter and your bill was only twenty cents. I'm positive that were the man, Sir!"

A strange light came over the older man's face, and he asked, "Are you through school, my Boy?" He looked Reggie in the eyes earnestly.

"No, not though; no, Sir. I can't go this year on account of my father's illness."

"But you like school!"

"Oh yes, Sir!" Said Reggie. I want to finish school, more than I can tell, but my father comes first."

The man reached out a trembling hand and took the worn nickel. His eyes got misty and his lip quivered.

"My boy." He said gently and sincerely, "for ten years I have been on the watch for a sincere, honest boy who is worthy of an education and can't afford it." Reggie's blood ran cold, and he gripped the counter.

"I had a son," he faltered; "he---he died. My only son, ---the pride and joy of my life. Smart, handsome, like his mother," The man drew out a handkerchief and wiped his eyes and face slowly.

"I had money laid up to send him through college, and I've never spent it. Seemed it was too sacred for me to spend it for a house, or a car, or comforts for myself. I promised him before he died, I'd send some good boy through school, but all the boys I thought would appreciate it did little things to prove to me they wouldn't appreciate it after all. I knew I had the nickel coming to me, my Boy. I heard you call, and I could have taken the next train for that matter; but I thought when you were cutting off that cheese you had an honest face, and you know I thought I'd just ---"

"Just what?"

"Put you to the test," spoke the man.

"Oh!" Reggie's face turned white, but hot, his breath came in great bunches that almost choked him.

"You see, Sir, my father was sick in the hospital for a long time---hurt in a car wreck, very badly---and I HAD to make good. Sir, there's a big bill to pay to yet, so I decided last night---I---I mean, God decided it for me. I knew I had to give up school this year for his sake. My dad, he's had a very hard time."

"Well, my Boy, you can plan to go. That little deal over the crackers and cheese told me a lot. I came back in here to see if you'd remember me."

"Sir, I never sold crackers and cheese, but that nickel in my pocket came to my mind."

"In which hospital is your father?"

"The Saint Mary's, Sir, on Fourth Street."

"Go with me after work; meet me at the corner,"

"Oh, Sir! First you must meet my father,"

"Does he know about the crackers and cheese?"

"I told him everything, that evening, Sir."

"Then, I know you are the boy that I have been looking for."

ON EASTER

By Christmas Carol Kauffman, age 38 Hannibal, Missouri
Originally published March 24, 1940
in the Youth's Christian Companion

John stopped abruptly as he entered the church. He must be late. They were singing.

"That was quite well done," her heard Brother Rendell say, "but the tenors come out a little stronger, especially on page fourteen. Now, let's go over that once more, beginning with "Christ's agony", it was---'at the bottom of page twelve. Now tenors, you sing out a little louder. I am sorry that John is not here today. We need him." He looked at the clock.

John hung up his coat and hat, and pressed down his hair. But instead of rushing in to take his place, he hesitated in the cloakroom. Something kept him back. "Christ's agony"---the chorus began once more softly, softly and with feeling. "It was for me," sang the sopranos, while the other parts hummed.

John could hear Velma's voice above the rest vibrate like a thin glass. It seemed to go to the ceiling and hang there trembling. John caught his breath, and held it. The chorus sang on and on the prelude to Christ's suffering and death,

"Deeper than tears is our despair,
Bitter than death the woe we share.
Hopes that rose high lie shattered asunder,
Gone is the friend so true---so tender."

John, standing there in semidarkness, felt a sudden loneliness sweep over him, a gnawing consciousness of some great emptiness, some sickening need he could not understand. The shadow in the cloakroom seemed to grow deeper and longer. He shivered. The music was fading now---fading slowly---ever so slowly away.

"Be seated, please," John heard Brother Rendlen say pleasantly. And they did. The walls of the cloakroom seemed to grow deeper and longer. He shivered again. He was standing close to the window that felt damp as if with liquid music. He wiped his forehead. His hand suddenly stopped the thought---he thought he heard some---, something strange. He listened, but heard nothing but the clock on the wall just inside the door.

Every face looked up as John entered briskly down the side isle. And found his place in the tenor section.

"John," spoke Brother Rendlen graciously, with his baton in mid air. "We are glad to have John here with us. Let us start once more from the beginning. I am well pleased with the progress you all are making, but there is still room for improvement. We have only one more practice before Easter. So let's do our best. Look closely please; ready. Just a minute. Peter switch on another light. There, that's better. Now let's try to feel the words and sing or best. If we want to make our message effective we must feel what we sing. Let us try to understand Our Savior Jesus Christ's sufferings, 'deeper than tears' ---"bitter than death'---broken in heart.

John looked at Velma, three seats away from him. Her blue dress made him even surer that he loved blue. Did she know? Oh, did she care just a little bit how much he cared?

"Page one. Attention please"

This time the chorus started out even more delicately and almost timidly, like tiny bells from over the halls, now louder, now softer, echoing and rejoicing from the mountains to the valley, and back again, then stronger and fuller, now more bells; larger bells, sad bells, sad soft bells. Once Velma's voice rang out above the rest.

John held his breath again. On and on they sang with John's rich tenor voice to help them. Then they sang though that solemn refrain on page fourteen.

Brother Rendlen smiled with satisfaction.

"Now then, when we begin on page seventeen, I would like you to sing more lightly, 'Rejoice ye sons of God.' Let's look happy and rejoice. Then hold it more firmly with the last refrain, 'Our Great Redeemer lives, the Lamb for sinners slain.' There is a wonderful message in this Easter Cantata. But not unless we get this powerful message across to our audience; our singing will all be in vain."

It was nine fifteen when Brother Rendlen told the choir good night. "All come back on Saturday afternoon at two promptly for our final rehearsal."

Velma wrapped and pulled her coat more tightly around her since it was so cold. Everyone was gone except for the janitor. He was in the basement and would want to be leaving very soon too. She stood shivering outside the choir door. There might be an Easter snowstorm. She looked toward the west. Oh, would he come? Cars---cars---, but not Roy's. If he did not come soon then she would start walking home. The janitor was coming out now with his car keys in his hand. He snapped out the light.

"Why, Velma, are you still here?"

"My brother was supposed to meet me here on his way home from work," was her dismal reply.

"Well, you'll get very cold standing out here."

"I'm mighty cold already. Say, if you don't mind, may I step inside and use the phone?"

"Certainly," And so saying, he snapped on the light. Velma ran to the phone in the vestibule. She stopped and stood cold and rigid and let out a stifled scream. On the floor under the back pew crumpled in a heap lay a child just waking from sleep. Her light curly hair was a mass of tangles. Bare knees shown through the torn stockings, and the lining of her coat, hung out in shreds. She made a frightened whimper, and big tears stood out in her tender blue eyes. Suddenly a surprised, almost faint smile crossed her face, and she crawled to her feet.

"Did you---did you---you all come to sing for me? She stammered.

Velma starred as though she has seen a ghost. "To---to sing for you? Little girl, what are you doing here and where did you come from?"

"Sudden fear seized the child. She shook frightfully. She suddenly looked away as though some horrible being might pounce out upon her from any corner.

"Where did you come from child?" The little thing was almost too frightened to answer.

"I---I don't know," she whispered, looking this way and that.

"You don't know?" Asked Velma lovingly.

The janitor was at the top of the steps now. The frightened little girl shook her shaggy head.

"I runned and runned till I got here."

"Why did you run?" Velma almost forgot she came in, intending to use the phone.

"I---I ranned away from Aunt Sarah. She---she" She faltered. "She got mad at me again, and told me if I wasn't going to beat it, she'd strap me---she would too!"

She was wiping the huge tears away now with her dirty coat sleeves making black streaks on her already grimy face.

"She straps you?" Asked Velma in a horrified voice.

"She's got a big, long strap---was Daddy's."

"Who is your daddy?" The child's eyes opened wider. "I ain't got one no more."

"Oh, did he die?" Velma's voice sounded padded. She shook her head, and then looked down quickly. Velma looked puzzled.

"He runned away, but Aunt Sarah says for me to tell folks, he's died."

"I---I see. And your mother?"

"She's---she's far away in a hospital, an' Aunt Sarah says she's just a lazy good-for-nothin' an' I's just a good for nothing nuisance, so I runned away too, till I got here."

"How did you get in?"

"Why, in the door, of course. I hearded the music and I crepted in to listen. T'was real pretty too. Oh, really swell. Made me feel lot safer. An, I jes' peeked over the topa those there benches a teeny bit so's none of you's could see me. I seen you up thar, lady, a singin so purty, but you's never looked at me onct. I stayed slidded down so's yous couldn't, cause I'd not paid ta come in, you see." The child chewed a little on her dirty fingers.

"Pay?" You don't need to ever pay to come to a church, little girl."

"Church? Oh my. I didn't knowed this was a church."

"Where did you think you were?" The janitor stood listening all the while, hat in hand.

"Why---I thought---I was in a—a—a--, is this a really, real church?" She looked all around wide eyed. "I always thoughted that they pray and read the Bible ina church, and I'd not heard any stuff like that---no prayin or readin."

"Well, dear, we were just practicing this evening for our Easter program next Sunday. We do read and pray in church here. Do you happen to know a lady by the name of Rosie Cookingham?

"Rosie Cookingham? She lives bied our house. And, a man in a big---big car comes and gets her everie Sunday mornin and takes her ta church, an brings her back, an Aunt

Sarah won't never let me go, cause she says Ida learn ta be good-for-nothin' likes my Mama. An, Rosie, she's a goin' ta speak a piece 'bout an angel rollin the stone a way, an' she's learned it all ta me, only Aunt Sarah doesn't know 'bout it. I wishth I could really go ta a real church just onct cause Rosie said its gona be Easter next Sunday. Is it gona be Easter here at this here church next Sunday too? An, that's tha songs ya were's singin for and practicin here what's ya goina sing next Sunday? And that's what's ya learnin them for tonight? Huh?"

The church door open and in stepped John Laurenson. He tipped his hat as Velma and the janitor looked around.

"Velma, I met Roy on my way home. He lost a wheel over on Maple Avenue, and I helped him to the garage. He told me to come after you and take you home so your folks won't worry." She coughed nervously. She was a little embarrassed.

"Where is Roy now?"

"At the garage, and who is that?" Asked John, pointing to the ragged child.

"Why, why!" He exclaimed as he looked at her a little more closely. "If it isn't little Nabby from Joliet Court! Nabby, how did you get over here?"

"I runned over."

"Do you know her?" Asked Velma with surprise.

"All I know is that my father goes around on Sunday mornings and gathers up several youngsters, and this looks like one he calls Nabby.

"Nabby, isn't that your name.? She nodded.

"How long have you been here?" Quickly Velma rehearsed the child's story and how she found her.

"Well, I thought I heard someone sobbing when I came in this evening but couldn't tell for sure at the time." John wished he hadn't said it—really he wished so. Quickly, Velma rehearsed the child's story and how she found her.

"Just think, John, she almost got locked up her for the night!"

"After this," remarked the Janitor, "I'd better---better", for some reason he did not finish what he started to say.

"Let's go, Come Nabby, we'll take you home if you don't tell me where you live."

"I---I---I don't want to go back there," she sobbed. Aunt Sarah will strap me—an' all I want to do is hear some more purty music."

"We'd better take you home, little girl!" Velma had her arms around her now. Oh, she was so thin and bony.

"You live in Joliet Court?" asked John. She nodded. Velma helped her in the front seat of the car, between herself and John.

The car stopped in front of what looked more like a shop rather than a house. Little Nabby was crying outright now, and clung frantically to Velma's coat.

"Don't cry, Nabby," she patted her arm gently. "I'll go inside and explain to your Aunt Sarah. You just sit here beside John till I come out. Don't cry."

Velma knocked on the door. The woman who came out was thin, thin, thin. She invited Velma to step inside.

The child in the car suddenly stopped crying and looked up into John's face.

"Who were you singin about tanight?" She asked nervously.

"Where?"

"In that there church?"

"Why---why, we were singing about Jesus." John coughed strangely and squirmed.

"Do you know who Jesus is?" John hesitated. "Do you know Him?"

"Not very much, sorta", came her quick reply.

"Rosie, she learns me some bout Him. Its bout Him that--that you's all were singin, bout, right? Its bout Him in that music your were singin bout and bout Him that she's gota speak bout for Easter? I don't think I'd knon Him if I happened ta see Him cause I'd never sawed Him. Have you ever seen Him?"

"No." John took his hat and put it back on.

"You never didn't? Well, don't He be there in church?" Rosie asked with great interest. Velma came out to the car, accompanied by her Aunt Sarah.

"It's alright, Nabby." She spoke tenderly, "Your Aunt Sarah will forgive you this time I think. And she promised to let you come along with Rosie to Sunday school next Sunday morning, and if you be real good, maybe you can come in the evening to hear the Easter music program too." Velma patted Nabby's dirty cheek tenderly.

"Oh, Aunt Sarah! Can I relly honesty Aunt Sarah? Oh, Aunt Sarah! Can I really honest, Aunt Sarah? Oh, I'd really promise ta sit right down and not maked a noise."

"Oh, never mind. Now Nabby, I didn't say for sure yet. Get out now an' come on ter bed. You got me 'bout skered ter death tonight. Come on Nabby, an' get out an come on in the house."

"Good night, Nabby: I hope to see you Sunday morning." Velma waved as they drove away.

"Bye, called Nabby.

"Strange things happen!" Said John.

"Don't they!" Added Velma.

"And thank you, John, for your trouble," said Velma cheerily as she got out in front of her home.

"Don't mention it, Velma. I was glad to do it for you." He looked after her longingly.

"Good night."

"Good night, Velma" She was gone far too soon.

Psychologists say that when we dream, the time element is very insignificant. An hour's drama may take place in a second, or a day's happenings in a minute. John dreamed all night, ---that is, all the part of the night that he slept. "Do you know Him, and did you ever see Him?" He woke with a start. Nabby was nowhere to be seen.

By nine o'clock on Easter morning the sun was shining. The Church was well filled when the first song was announced. A hush fell over the audience when the superintendent got up.

"First of all." He said, "Rosie Cookinghan will speak a piece, 'On Easter Morning', what is it?" He was bending over and Rosie was whispering something in his ear. "Well", he announced, smiling as he said it, "Well, playmate Nabby, will speak with her."

One could have heard a pin drop as the two little girls, in worn faded dresses, but very evident shining faces, repeated together their Easter recitation. Several wiped away tears because of the tenderness that shone on their faces.

At the close of the program the minister stepped to the edge of the platform and said, "I feel like extending an invitation this morning. Perhaps there is one soul here this morning who has never yet accepted Jesus as their Savior and Redeemer. Perhaps there is someone here who has accepted Him, but has not been enjoying victory as he'd like to, or someone who feels like making an even more change in your personal walk and talk with the Lord. If there is a person in this congregation today, I extend a special invitation. Just stand and make it known.

One young man in the back of the room stood. It was John Laurenson.

In the evening the church was packed. The Easter Cantata was rendered perfectly. Brother Rendlen was pleased because of the spirit of the Lord that was abundant.

"John," someone touched him gently on the arm. John turned and looked Velma straight into the eyes.

"I'm glad you stood this morning. I---I ---hoped you would."

"You did?"

"I have for a long time." She looked down.

"You have?" He seemed surprised.

"Yes," she looked up.

"Why?"

"I can't tell you now."

"When will you then?"

"When I have---"

"A chance?" John touched her arm. She looked down and blushed a little.

"I'll give you a chance, if you'll let me take you home." Her breath came fast. She fumbled with her purse strap neverously.

"Oh, Velma, his voice was rich and low. His eyes shone with a true sincerity she had never before seen in John Laurenson's eyes, "You've turned me down so often, and I don't blame you, Velma. Everything can be different now. I feel like I really felt the presence of Jesus last night and I want his influence in my life. I can't forget you. I never cared for anyone else like I care for you."

"Neither have---"she caught herself. Oh, what was she saying anyway? It was something she hoped that she might, some day, be saying to him.

"Velma!" They walked out together; hand in hand.

OUT OF THE DEPTHS

By Christmas Carol Kauffman, age 40 Hannibal, Missouri
Originally published March 9, 16 and 23, 1942
in the Youth's Christian Companion

Personal comments by the Editor of the C. F. Yake, Editor

The forces of sin are making tremendous inroads upon young people of our country, and in the homes of all classes. The devil is no respecter of persons either, in seeking the destruction of souls. The winning of souls to Jesus Christ, and the saving of them for Christ, ere sin has worked havoc, is no small task for Christian workers, parents, teachers, ministers, and evangelists; for with such work, goes also the great task of fortifying the believers with the Word of God through Christian instruction. And while we want our own to be reared in the knowledge of the Word of God, which is not the limit of our responsibility; for those who belong to others are ours too, by His grace. Let us be diligent in this great task of evangelism.

For obvious reasons, the characters and the setting of this story of the havoc of sin, and the saving grace of our Lord and Savior, within His grace, and attending blessings, are camouflaged by the author. This is a true story. May we pray together that this message may be a means of awakening us to realize more keenly our responsibilities and opportunities to testify of Jesus Christ.

***

A strange hush like a sudden benediction fell over the audience as the young woman entered. She neither slammed the door nor did she make noise as she came down the isle. She hesitated a moment, then took a seat beside a middle-aged woman in gray. The minister behind the pulpit took the Bible in his hand and, stepping to the edge of the platform, spoke in a rich voice.

"Let us come before the Lord in prayer. With these precious thoughts upon our minds, let us get a hold of Jesus, our Lord and Redeemer tonight with new understanding and with fresh courage and greater faith. Anyone, please feel free to pray as the Spirit leads."

The minister knelt behind the railing around the sacred platform; and as he did so, the congregation knelt likewise. The young woman caught her breath. Should she kneel too? The little woman in gray at her side did, everyone did but the girl. She had never knelt in church before or at home, or anywhere she could remember. She noticed that a heavyset man across the isle was keeping his seat and just bowing his head; so she bowed hers also.

A man close to the front began to call on the name of the Lord in such a familiar way, that the girl could hardly believe her ears. "Get a hold of God" she thought. "Why, why can that man pray as if God had a hold of him, and he liked it, and they really understood each other?" Then a woman from somewhere near the front, prayed aloud with such a soft delicate voice that the girl could scarcely hear her; but somehow she could feel that she was truly sincere, and had done it often before.

Then a young girl prayed, and how she pled for a Sister Bean who was in the hospital! But then, when the little lady in gray prayed, the girl's whole body felt warm, and with her hand over her eyes, she trembled; a good trembling feeling inside. She had never been that close to a person who was praying to God. The woman's clear voice broke when she prayed for her wayward son and his little boy who were both, so sick. "They must really love that little fellow," thought the girl to herself, "If I only had a grandmother who loved me and knew how to pray." A tear trickled down her cheek. She brushed it away quickly. Here and there young and old led out in prayer, and at last the minister closed that part of the service.

"Now, if some of you folks," began the minister, "want to tell the rest of us about some definite and remarkable answers to prayer you've had recently, and can tell it to the honor and glory of God, I'll give you the opportunity. Who'll be first?"

A small man with white hair rose and told how the good Lord had saved his life in an accident at the factory that very day. A heavy-set woman told how she had plead to the Lord, and searched so long and how the Lord had given her work to earn enough to pay rent and she knew it was a blessing of paying a full and honest tithe. A young man told how his cousin for whom he had been praying for several years found Jesus Christ on what he thought was going to be his death bed.

The young stranger sat nervously. She leaned forward. At the close of the service, and the minister hurried to the vestibule to shake hands with the people as they left.

"Good evening," he held out his hand and smiled sincerely, "What is your name?" The girl held out her thin hand.

"My name," she hesitated, is Dorothy Osborn." She blushed slightly as she said it, and shifted from one foot to the other. She was grateful to be there and at the same exact time was very nervous, for some reason.

"My name is White. You've never been here before?"

"No sir, never before."

"Do you live in town?"

"Yes, sir, I do." Her eyes dropped. She was rather shy.

"I hope you enjoyed the service tonight. Please do come back again, Miss Osborn.

"Thank you," the girl took a step forward and stopped. She turned halfway around.

"Do you---"she began.

"Ma'am?" The minister bent forward in kindness and concern. The people in the isle and vestibule were visiting. The minister was very friendly. He was already shaking hands with Sister DeWitt.

"Just a minute, Miss. You said something I did not understand. I'm sorry." The girl looked the minister straight in the face, "I was told that you folks here pray for sick people."

"Yes, we sure do!"

"And they are healed?"

"Well." Brother White stroked his hair slowly and smiled. "We do pray for those that are sick, to be sure. We pray for all the needs of mankind. Especially the individuals we know about personally.

"Oh!"

He thought he read deep concern in her voice. She looked down, and fumbled with her purse strap. "I wonder if I came to the wrong---"For some reason she could not finish her sentence. Hadn't she heard those ferverent prayers?

"You say you were told by someone that we pray for the sick, and they are **always** healed?"

"I thought that's what she said, or at least meant to say," she looked up again.

"May I ask who told you that?"

"Well, the laundry lady. You see---"she drew a long breath and caught the edge of the post for support. The minister noticed that her lip trembled; in fact her entire body seemed suddenly to quiver like a leaf on a tree.

"You see," she began again, "I'm sick. Very, very sick. The doctor told me last week I haven't long to live. I called him up---I pretended to be an aunt from out of town, who really wanted to know the truth about my nieces condition--- you see. I felt she was keeping things from me, (the doctor, you know). My folks don't know I called him or---or what he said. He even told me over the phone not to let them know it, my folks, and do everything to keep up the girl's spirits." A sickening smile played around her lips.

"Do sit down, Miss Osborn. Come have a seat until I shake hands with a few more folks and I'll talk with you." She sat down. Soon he was beside her.

"And then what?" He asked.

"Well, you can imagine how I felt. You see, I am the only child and my father is well fixed. I was brought up in society and, I know---"She bent forward and dropped her hands wearily on her lap.

"I know I'm dying---dying---because of my wild life. I never was robust. I just couldn't stand it, ---the fast life. My parents don't like to admit that, however. But I know it is true. My friends have been sending me gifts of all descriptions, but it is a bunch of "balony" to me. It does not satisfy. It doesn't even help when you know---you know you haven't a long time to live."

She stopped for a moment to catch her breath. Her face was white, and dark rings gave a distinct shadow below her eyes.

"Last week when Sal---"she coughed, "I mean, when our laundry lady came, I sent word down for her to come up to my room. She always seemed so happy for some reason, peaceful, I mean, and often I could hear her singing in the basement as she worked---the songs were of Jesus and his love and concern for us, so I called her up and told her my terrible secret! And she told me about you people here in this church, and how you pray for folks and they are healed. So, I thought---I thought I would perhaps---"

"That perhaps you could be healed?" Asked the minister.

"Do you---you think---?" She asked anxiously. He replied quickly.

"All things are possible---we believe in the Lords will and always accept his plan for each of us. We must believe, because He knows all."

"Sister, not everyone we have prayed for has been healed, however. I'll be honest with you. We must pray for the Lord's will to be done." He waited, and then asked gently,

"Are you a Christian, Miss Osborn?"

"Well---well, I've never really gone to church, except once or twice, for a funeral and a few times on Easter and just before Thanksgiving and Christmas. Oh, my folks don't know I came over here tonight. Oh, if they knew they would have fits! They went to a party and sent for a friend of mine to come and stay with me to, jolly me up. And after they left, I called her and told her I didn't need her to come tonight. Then I got dressed and called a taxi. I want to get back home before my parents come." She looked at the clock. It was 9:15 pm.

"Oh, they won't be home for a long time yet." She gave a sigh. "They would be furious if they knew this; that I am here of all places, and so would the doctor; but I thought if I could---"She stopped abruptly, while a wistful, pitiful, troubled expression crossed her tired face.

"Sister," The minister spoke so tenderly it almost startled her. "First of all, do you truly want to find peace?" He waited for an answer, but none came. A red spot appeared on each pale cheek, and he noticed her eyes were misty.

"Don't you?" He asked at length. He waited.

"Oh, if I only knew how! Sir, I am ashamed to tell you how positively ignorant I am about such things. My parents have faithfully taught me to do anything and everything to keep myself popular with the wrong crowd. I have studied the fashion plates. I could not even repeat the Lord's Prayer if you paid me to. Religion has never been a part of my life. I know there is a God and I know there are people who know how to pray; I heard them tonight. I'm so sick that I thought I couldn't even come here tonight, but for some reason I ---some unexplainable reason---some unexplainable force---some spirit, or something made me do it. Was I silly? I never heard such powerful, sincere prayers, sir. In fact, it was all so wonderful to me. Oh, if I only knew how. I---I---if I must die..."Her voice broke. "I must have God go with me!"

"Listen, Miss Osborne," spoke the minister finally. I know you are sick. You must be very tired. My wife didn't come to church today because the baby was rather cross from cutting teeth; but I'll tell you what we'll do. Could we both come to your home tomorrow afternoon and take plenty of time to explain it all to you and answer any questions you may have?"

"Oh, ---Oh!" The girl cut him off. She stood up; stood up straight. "No, that would never do. Please don't come to my home. I will come back here when I have a chance."

"Do you have a Bible?"

"I'm not sure if there even is one in the house or not."

"Just a minute." The minister hurried to a side room and soon was back with a Bible in his hand.

"I'll mark what I'd like for you to read. Promise me that you'll read what I have marked as soon as possible. And read it over several times."

"I will," she answered.

He handed her the Bible that was marked in the Gospel according to John. "We are saved by faith and faith cometh by hearing, and hearing by the Word of God. So first of all, I'd like you to begin, by reading the Word of God and then pray as you read so the Holy Ghost can reveal to you, its truthfulness, and the Holy Spirit, which we also call it, will reveal to you its truthfulness and help you believe, and to understand its simple message. I promise you that we will pray for you through your grave illness. Will that be alright?" She nodded. Her face was still wet with tears.

"Our next service here will be on Thursday night at 7:30. I will be looking for you.

"And I surely will be here if I can. Is there a phone here so I can call a taxi?" She looked around.

"Not here, I'm sorry. But I will step across the street, and call one for you."

"Thank you so very much."

Daniel White closed the church door softly as the taxi drove away. He prayed as he watched it turn the corner.

"Is Johnnie asleep?" Daniel White asked as opened the cottage door.

"Yes, Dan. You are rather late tonight."

"Come, sit here beside me and I'll tell you why." She complied without being coaxed.

"Didn't we pray that the Lord would bring some hungry soul to church tonight? Well, He did, Evelyn. Such a troubled, very ill, pitiful girl. After I've told you, you will pity her too." Then he shared everything in detail to his wife.

Thursday evening came, but Dorothy Osborn was not at church. Brother White watched the door each time someone entered. But the girl with the overwhelming burden did not come and Pastor White felt a burden for her also. The congregation of saints offered her case up before the Lord. Bro.White had given the new prayer request for all the members to specifically pray for Dorothy Osborn.

Sunday evening came. Again, Brother White entered the chapel door hoping for Dorothy Osborn: but the pale faced girl did not show up. Was she worse? He wondered. Perhaps she's at deaths door? He watched the papers carefully. He scanned the telephone book. There was an Osborn junk dealer. That would not be her father. He knew he wasn't. Mr. Osborn the MeNess dealer; he knew him. There was an Osborn undertaker; a J. C. Osborn and a Fannie Osborn. He called at least a dozen numbers inquiring for a girl named Dorothy, but no one seemed to know a girl by the name of Dorothy. He called the Public Library and asked if a Dorothy Osborn had a card.

"No", said the librarian. "We have a David Osborn, a Martha Osborn, and a Lou Osborn, but no Dorothy has a card."

"Thank you."

"Evelyn, why didn't I ask her where she lived?"

"You really should have. Just pray that she will come back. Do you suppose she is a fake?"

"A fake? I can hardly believe that. If she was, she surely was good at acting.

***

Dorothy did come the following Thursday night. The service was nearly half over, when the taxi stopped in front of the Church. Softly she closed the door. Brother White was speaking from the 16th chapter of Acts, about the jailer who would have committed suicide, but the Lord intervened.

Shall I take my life to avoid trouble and disgrace? He was saying, or shall I give my life to God, and let Him save me from the disgrace of sin? Shall I blot out my own life or let God help me, by giving me the strength I need to be able blot out my sins and make my life useful? Some people today, like the fear-stricken jailer, would draw the sword, but Jesus Christ offers each of us a better way."

He picked up a song book, and read with feeling:

"Out of my bondage, sorrow and night
Jesus, I come; Jesus I come;
Into Thy freedom, gladness and light
Jesus, I come to Thee:
Out of my sickness, unto thy health,
Out of my want and into Thy wealth,
Out of my sin and into Thyself,
Jesus, I come to thee."

Dorothy Osborn sat breathless. The church was cool with autumn rain in the air, but her face was hot.

"Out of my shameful failure and loss,
Jesus, I come; Jesus to thee."
Into the glorious gain of Thy cross,
Jesus, I come to thee."
Out of earth's sorrows and into thy balm,
Out of life's storms and into Thy calm,
Out of distress to jubilant psalm,
Jesus, I come to Thee."

Brother White saw the girl wipe her forehead with her handkerchief. How he longed to help her! But what more comforting words could he find then these God had marvelously directed his hands to find?

"Out of unrest and arrogant pride,
Jesus, I come; Jesus I come;
Into Thy blessed will I'll abide,
Jesus I come to thee."
Out of myself to dwell in Thy love,
Out of despair into raptures above,
Upward for aye on wings like a dove,

Jesus, I come to Thee."

Dorothy dropped a kid glove on the floor. She let it lie there.

"Out of the fear and dread of the tomb.
The girls head dropped low.
Jesus, I come; Jesus I come."

Her breath came faster.

"Into the joy and light of Thy home,
Jesus, I come to thee."
She drew a big sigh.
"Out of the depths of ruin untold,
Into the peace of Thy sheltering fold.
Ever Thy glorious face to behold,
Jesus, I come to Thee."

"Let us pray." Heads went down and Dorothy Osborn's was already down. When Brother Winters leads in prayer, he always asks if there is anyone who wants' to be remembered in prayer" Just raise your hand and we will pray for you."

Brother Winters prayed. Two hands went up. One was thin and white.

"I would like to speak to the two who raised their hands for prayer. After the service is dismissed, will you please remind me to speak to you?"

The benediction was pronounced. Brother White went directly to Mr. Henderson and lifted his hand. He talked with him about ten minutes.

Dorothy Osborn just kept her seat. She seemed not to have enough strength to get up. A number of folks shook hands with her, and she looked too tired and too sad to visit much with anyone.

"I am so glad that you got here tonight." The pastor took her hand and shook it very gently. "Did you read your Bible?"

"Yes, I hid it under my mattress."

"We looked for you last Thursday night and again on Sunday.

"Oh, I just couldn't manage it. So much company." She shook her head. "I almost had to---well, it was very hard for me to get here tonight."

"Meet Sister White, Miss Osborn."

"I am so happy to meet you, Miss Osborn."

"Thank you, I am glad to meet you too."

"We have been praying for you ever single day in our home." Said the minister's wife.

"Thank you: I am very happy to meet you. She repeated. Thank you, I really appreciate it."

"And why did you raise your hand tonight, Miss Osborn?" Brother White asked.

"Oh, Brother, I am so wretched. I know I need something only God can give. I know it, but to decide to break away, ---oh, you can't even know how hard it would be. My home, my friends, I would disgrace the family. No, you wouldn't."

"Listen to this." No man that has left house or parents or brethren, or wife, or children, for the kingdom of God's sake, who shall receive manifold; more in this present time, and in the world to come which brings us life everlasting." Dorothy sat in deep thought.

"I will read it again." Slowly, the minister read those very words the Master told Peter one day." Still, Dorothy sat.

"Is it really, really true?" she asked in all sincerity.

"God cannot lie, my friend. Just try Him out. If He fails, I'll quit preaching. He's never once failed me. He wants to help you. That's why He has called you to come out where you can hear His word. Has it helped you any to have been here tonight?"

"Oh, I don't know. I feel so weak in my body. I am failing, and I can't fool myself into believing I'm not. I know my days are numbered. I think the folks see it. They lavish every kind of luxury on me. Today my father had ten fur coats delivered to the house and told me to pick out one I wanted. Fur coat indeed! I'll never need one. If he only knew what I wanted---peace to my soul. But I can't tell him. I know they would think I had lost my mind entirely. They have been wanting to send me to a hospital. But I object with all my heart. The nurse bores me to tears sometimes. She is so shallow and empty. She thinks I am getting queer, because I don't talk, but I---I can't." She stopped to rest.

"I really must go. I mustn't keep you two any longer. Will you please call a taxi again for me---."

"Let's take you home. It is raining and we'd be glad...."

"No indeed. Please call a taxi. I wouldn't want to bother you."

"But, we'd be glad to," put in Sister White.

When Dorothy Osborne shook her head they knew she meant so. Somehow, they just knew it.

"Before you leave, well pray for you, Miss Osborn. We'll ask God to help you give your heart, your life, your love, your affection---everything you have, ---your father, your mother, your friends, and **everything,** over to Him. Is that what we should pray for?"

The clock on the east wall ticked and ticked. The girl held one hand tight in the other. Her shoulders rose and fell like one would, under a great soul burden. The baby in Sister

White's arms whimpered. The girl seemed not to bear it. A tear fell on her hands, ---a large tear, that could not be held back any longer. Sometimes seconds seemed like hours. The clock just kept ticking.

If I didn't love my wife here," the minister's voice was warm and gentle, "more than any other woman in the world, Dorothy, what kind of love would you call it?"

"Why, I wouldn't even call it love," came her quick reply.

"Then unless we love God above everything else, we don't love Him at all."

Dorothy Osborn looked up. Her muscles relaxed and a faint smile crossed her tearstained face.

"Pray," she whispered, at length.

The three knelt on the bare church floor, while the minister prayed. He prayed until great beads of perspiration stood out.

"Do you care to pray for yourself, Miss Osborn, while we're here alone?"

Now, Brother Daniel White never liked to coax or beg anyone. He read several other Scriptures to her and then called a taxi.

"Where do you live?"

If Dorothy heard Sister White's question---well, she never let on.

Soon she was gone again. Almost like a dream, ---in she came and out again. Some dreams are forgotten before breakfast. Some remain throughout the day; but Dorothy Osborn and the dream she brought lingered more than a day, more than two days.

***

It was Sunday night, twelve days later. Brother White had finished his sermon, and had extended an invitation. The congregation was singing the last verse of the song,

"Come---Out of the Depths of ruin untold---." The door opened and in stepped Dorothy. She paused for a moment, then stood in the lobby, listening and then --- then staggering up the isle of the church, she sank on the front seat of the chapel and buried her face in her hands.

"God bless you Dorothy, the minister repeated. Then a number of people who carried concern for her burdened hungry soul, gathered around her for prayer, including the loving, tenderhearted pastor.

"Brother White," Dorothy Osborn's voice faltered. "I want to take upon Jesus Christ as my Savior tonight and learn more and more about His love for me and my broken heart. I feel so lost and burdened down, but I must make a confession. I am not Dorothy Osborn. I don't know anyone by that name. I am Charlotte McDaniel. My father is the banker, Arthur McDaniel."

A hush fell over the small concerned group of friends, gathered around her. All eyes opened wide. All eyes and hearts felt love for this lonely girl, needing a friend, but especially a friend in Jesus. She smiled and stood there.

"I---I was afraid---and ashamed to let you all know who I really was---or to be honest, I was afraid to have any of my friends find out that I have been coming to this little church. There's Billie Blain." She said nodding to the woman that stood beside her smiling with love in her eyes, "she's been our laundry lady for years and---and she promised me that if I'd come here, she would never let anyone know and also not let anyone know that she knew me. She's the one who told me about how you people pray for others and help others, and so---" she wrung her hands and drew a long breath.

"I---I, Brother White, I can't keep it a secret any longer as to who I really am. I told my parents today where I was going and what I intend to do. They stormed, of course. That's why I never got here much. They think I have gone mad and am completely ruined socially. If I have, I can't help it. I know I'm ready to die soon and need to be ready. I can't face death the way I am. I really must decide once and for all if I am for or against --- Jesus Christ---and I **must** know it for sure. Brother White, Brother White, will you please forgive me for lying to you about who I told you, I was?" She looked at him in such a childlike pleading way.

"Certainly---certainly, Miss Osbo---I mean Miss McDaniel."

"I know you have often seen my picture in the paper, but I have changed so much since I'm sick, Oh---Oh, I so much want peace tonight. I can't," she cried, "I can't stand this any longer! I've gone to the depths of sin and the last few weeks I have been in the depths of agony that no one knows about. Oh, I want to find peace in my heart, before I die!" She dropped on her knees and began to cry unto Heavenly Father for his mercy and grace.

He did hear her sincere plea; her penitent prayer and by faith she found freedom within her soul that was sincerely searching for light and truth. That night. from the depths of sorrow, she came to a glorious understanding of light and truth of the Saviors atoning sacrifice that could heal her wounded heart and soul. She knew that she could find Joy Unspeakable.

Charlotte McDaniel came to every service after that. Although she was severely ridiculed by her old friends and by their parents, she continued to attend the little church where she found the tender compassionate love of her Lord and Savior Jesus Christ.

Her jewels disappeared, and she found the true jewels of the truth in the scriptures. Her step became lighter; her pale cheeks took on a natural tint, and one evening she came walking to church with her Bible in her hands. The peace of God which passeth all understanding flooded her face as she spoke to Brother White at the door.

"Brother White,' she said radiantly, "Do you know, I truly believe that God has healed me."

"Praise the Lord, Charlotte! You are looking ever and ever so much better."

"I am better, Brother White. I walked to church tonight; think of it, twelve blocks! I was so thrilled over finding truth, I asked God to heal my broken body and heal my wounded soul." Her voice was sincerely grateful.

"It is just His great love and concern for our soul, dear sister. Didn't I tell you that He never, ever fails us? As we truly seek Him and His divine guidance in our lives, He leads us every step of the way. He promises us that if we leave house and parents and everything for Him, we will receive manifold blessings, more in this present time and also in the world to come, which is everlasting life.

"Oh, it is all so marvelous, Brother White!"

Several years later Charlotte McDaniel became the wife of Samuel Cluffen. Although he is not as enthusiastic about the Lord's work as Charlotte is, he is a good and kind husband and a prosperous business man. All her needs are supplied. And she gives of her material blessings to the Lord. Many persons have been blessed by her honest and testimony. They now have three daughters. Recently Sister Cuffen made this statement in a prayer meeting:

"Friends, I have been serving the Lord now for twenty-five years, and I love Him more every day. I trust His promises more every day. I can truly testify that He saves, He forgives, He heals, and He keeps His promises to us as we dedicate our lives to Him and His will for each of you. But it is also true that as you sow, so shall you reap. I am reaping today what I sowed over twenty years ago; for tonight while I am here enjoying this blessed fellowship with others who love the Lord with all their heart as I truly do, I can testify of His healing of each of hearts and souls and minds. Please pray for my daughter Grace, that somehow the she will allow the Lord to be a part of her life too as He has done for me. I believe with all my heart that He will as she allows him to come into her life. I praise the Lord that my one daughter has accepted the Savior into her life, but I am heavy burdened for my other daughter. She needs the Lord Jesus in her life as desperately as I needed Him in my life, many years ago. Just as truly as the Lord Jesus drew me close to Him as I accepted His grace in my life, I know that He can bring my daughter out of the depths of unrighteousness into a new life in Christ Jesus as we plead for her to accept His saving grace. I know He is able to change the life of Grace as she is willing to humble herself into His divine will for her, exactly as He has done for me. So please, please pray for her as all of you have done for me."

A BOY

By Christmas Carol Kauffman, age 32 Hannibal, Missouri
Originally published November 21, 1934
in the Youth's Christian Companion

There are homes without boys, parents living alone,
And many a good boy is without a good home.
But the one I am praying for both night and today,
The one that I care for in a very special way'
is the boy who is good, both ambitious and true,
Who has a good home, and is obedient too
Yet, he lacks but one thing, only one thing I say,
And it's the greatest of all, in every single way.
It's the boy without God, as a brother and chum.
Who has never said "yes" to His call, "Won't you come?"
That is the boy, dear Lord, for whom I do pray
We'll add to his life, what he's lacking today.

WORD POSSIBLE

When I was young, Mother created a game that we played in our home. We call the game *Word Possible--A Game with over Twelve Thousand Possible Answers* will soon be published and available through Digital Legend Press

Ten reasons this game will be a favorite in your home and family

1. Develops Creative Thinking skills.
2. Can be played with all ages.
3. Good Healthy competition.
4. Different each time it is played.
5. Develops memory skills for both young and old.
6. A great family game and can be played any where.
7. Can be played with any number of players
8. Can be minutes or hours of fun.
9. Brings happiness to all- a circle of joy.
10. The game is forever playable even if cards are lost.

A FUN EASY Game for all ages

* A Question & Answer Game Using Letters of Alphabet
* Great for Family or Friend Reunions
* Large or Small Groups
* Can Take Anywhere
* Easy & Challenging
* Over 15,000 "Possible" Answers

Players: 2 +

Object of Game:
Have fun with other players, calling out answers to categories. Player with the most cards wins the game.

The game will release in 2012 and be available through a variety of channels and resellers including direct-order from the publisher Digital Legend Press.

Dial 877-222-1960 for more information.

Marcia Kauffman Clark is the youngest of Nelson Edward and Christmas Carol Kauffman's four children. She moved with her parents and brother James Milton, to Elkhart, Indiana in August 1956. Marcia sang in a sextet with the same six girls all four years while attending Bethany Christian High School in Goshen, Indiana. She attended Hesston College in Hesston Kansas for two years and graduated with a Secondary Education Degree in Home Economics in 1965 from Goshen College, Goshen, Indiana. The greatest highlight of her high school and college years was singing and especially with the traveling choirs while in college. Marcia moved to Phoenix, Arizona, in 1969. She has enjoyed teaching, singing, sewing, and creative writing. She sang first alto in a ladies quartette for twenty-one years. She had the opportunity of traveling in Europe twice as a ten-year member of the Sonoran Desert Chorale. She and her husband, Stephen, live in Tempe, Arizona, and have eight children, twenty-two grandchildren, and one great-grandson.

Marcia Kauffman Clark can be reached by mail at:

1026 East Alameda Drive

Tempe, Arizona 85282

e-mail: mkauffmanclark@gmail.com

The Carol of Christmas
Life Story of Christmas Carol Kauffman

Comin' Home Soon
And Other Short Stories Vol 1

In the Time of Lilacs
And Other Short Stories Vol 2

Watch for the entire collection of Christmas Carol Kauffman books written and compiled by Carol's youngest daughter Marcia. Order any of the above by dialing toll free: **877-222-1960** or by sending check or money order for $16.95 each to:

Digital Legend 1994 Forest Bend Dr. Cottonwood Hts, UT 84121

www.ingramcontent.com/pod-product-compliance
Lightning Source LLC
Chambersburg PA
CBHW051652260626
47170CB00004B/1459